DE

Danielle Marcus
&
Wilzo

Diamond Dior Publications

Dmpnovels@gmail.com

First Printing May 2019
Printed in the United States of America

10 9 8 7 6 5 4 3 2 1

Distributed by Danielle Marcus Presents, LLC.
Submit wholesale orders to:
daniellemarcuspresents@yahoo.com
Phone: (248)284-3903

Dedication

Seventeen years of knowing just how to push each other's buttons, when a smile is needed to brighten each other's day, and when to give each other our space creates a bond that I never knew was possible. Two kids and two books came out of the deal, so I guess you're not that bad. Lol. Relationships doesn't come with a handbook... at least, I know ours didn't. No matter where this crazy world takes us, you'll always have a place in my heart. This book is dedicated to our teamwork in actually getting it done. Nigga, we made it!!

Chapter One

Oxy

“Wake this bitch up.”

I felt the sting on my left cheek as a hand landed across it. I didn’t recognize his voice and as my eyes slowly peeled open, I let out a groan, attempting to clear my groggy throat. It was on fire and my temple was throbbing. I felt like I’d been hit by a truck. Where the hell was I? Where was Dre? I needed my man.

Confusion turned into anger as my gaze lifted to two masked men. Everything began to flood my memory at once... Pops. The nigga hiding in my backseat. Shit, someone had gotten down on me.

My hands were bound. I couldn’t move my feet. Now, I was beginning to panic. Who were they and what the fuck did they want?

“Where the rest of the money?” The deep, raspy voice snapped me out of my thoughts.

‘What money?” I frowned, wishing I could apply pressure to relieve some of the tension pounding in my head.

He let out a small laugh. “You still playing tough, huh?” He stood over me, taunting me. “That’s why you got knocked the fuck out the first time.”

My lips tightened. “When Dre finds you. He's going to kill you,” I whispered, praying for my baby. I needed him now more than ever. I promise, if I made it out alive, I was going to listen to him. He told me not to pick up the bag and I should have listened.

The man jumped at me. His fist stretched back, but his friend stopped him. “Yo', chill nigga. Let's see what Manny want us to do. The bitch can’t talk if you kill her. The fuck you keep hitting ‘dis girl for anyway?”

“Because she got too much fuckin' mouth. Think this shit a game. End up floating in the Detroit river with the fishes.” He snatched his arm free. “Don’t worry about what the fuck I’m doing, soft ass nigga.”

I scanned the room as they began to argue, searching for a weapon, an escape, or some piece of hope. There was nothing. It was modernly furnished; flat screens, a sectional, and a bookshelf. We were in somebody's house.

“Nah, you on some hoe shit. Dawg said grab the bag and dip.”

“Well, Man said snatch her up and get a bigger bag. So, this bitch gon' take us to it.”

“Where that nigga at now?”

“Picking his sister up,”

I listened to them talking loosely, wondering who the hell Man was. I heard the name before, but I couldn’t place where. Maybe my adrenaline was too high to even attempt to try.

A cell phone rang and I watched the fuck boy that tried to hit me pull it to his ear. He talked for a minute or two before ending the call. “Yo’, Man said take her to Sunny’s crib. He about to pull up with Sis and he don’t want her all in our business.”

“Yo', you a dumb ass, nigga. The fuck you keep saying names for?”

“Because it don’t matter, Tone.” Dude chuckled, as if it was a joke.

Obviously, Tone didn’t find it funny. He stepped into ol’ boy’s face. “Well, the way I see it, CJ. If I have to kill this bitch because she knows everybody’s name, I’m gon’ save a bullet for your punk ass too.”

Alarm settled in and rang through my body like a beacon. I wanted to tell them that I didn’t remember nobody’s name. However, that traumatized little girl inside of me wouldn’t allow myself to be weak. Even if I was scared shitless, I couldn’t let them know it.

***

Sunny

“What the fuck I’m supposed to do with her?” I ran my hands over my face, frustrated. All these simple niggas had to do was watch for the drop and snatch the bag. That’s all I gave him the task to do.

“Bro, do you know how much money we would be leaving on the table if we just let her walk away? Think nigga.”

I felt the muscles in my jaw begin to pull. Obviously CJ forgot who the fuck I was. My eyes traveled to the broad bound and gagged, laying on my basement floor, then to my soldier. Before he could blink, I grabbed him up and slammed him against the wall. "So you call the shots, nigga? You the one running shit now, huh?" I gritted, keeping a strong hold on his neck, applying pressure.

"Nah, Sunny. I,"

Grabbing the pistol off my waist, I clocked him upside his head. Hopefully it would knock some sense into his rock head. "The fuck you saying my name for and you got this bitch all up in my crib, about to start a war that I ain't got time to fight. You do what the fuck I say, nigga. You don't make your own decisions!"

I was seeing red. When CJ called and told me the drop was made and a female picked it up alone, I just knew we had made out with an easy lick. My pistol landed across his head again before I released him. Fuck up.

"Aight. Wait, man." CJ pleaded. "Hear me out, boss. I was thinking about us. Man told me to do it. Do you know how much money they been getting? We been watching the spot for a minute, bro." He let out a groan, rubbing the side of his head. "There was only a few bands in that bag. But I know with this broad, we can make away with enough bread to set us off right. D-low said they was pulling in a hundred thousand a week before he disappeared. He said all we had to do was get the drop on the bitch and we good. She run all that shit. I wasn't trying to be on no slime ball shit, bro." He pleaded, holding his hands up in surrender.

I thought about D-Low. He had bragged about the sweet ass lick he was setting us up for. Then, he just disappeared one day. I figured he had pulled off the lick without us. But, I got word that he got his ass cancelled. The lick wasn't as sweet as he made it seem and here this nigga was kidnapping a broad and bringing her back to my shit. He didn't have a clue who followed him, who was tracking her phone… I shook my head, walking over to the broad. I leaned down, grabbing her pockets for her cell. I wasn't taking no chances on her having that where's my I-phone shit for them niggas to be running up in my crib.

She began to scream, attempting to scoot out my reach. This shit wasn't my style. I wasn't no motherfuckin' kidnapper, no killer, or no rapist. I was a jack boy. We took nigga's shit and got the fuck on.

"Where her phone at, nigga? Did you shake her down?"

CJ nodded. "Hell yeah. All her shit at Man-Man crib. He told me to bring her here until we figured something out."

I blew out a stressed breath of air, too frustrated to decipher this shit. Man Man was my right hand. We started the crew together. I trusted his decisions, but I wasn't feeling him making them without me.

"Just make sure she tied up secure. Y'all motherfuckas not about to stress me out tonight. Why the fuck y'all didn't just keep her at his crib?"

CJ shrugged. "Because Kelsey was there. You know he think his sister God or some shit."

I'm not about to go down with this dumb nigga. We gon' have to kill this broad because she know all our names now. I kneaded at my temple, deciding to call up, Man Man. He had to get this broad up out my crib.

Chapter Two

Dre

"Don't even try it, bitch. Didn't yo' daddy teach you to lock doors..." The voice kept replaying in my head. I had called Ox's phone a million times and still no answer.

I was always ready for war. But, this shit right here... it wasn't part of the game. The rules had just changed and for whoever that voice belonged to, for his sake, I prayed my ears were deceiving me.

There's certain shit that a man just didn't want to hear... didn't want to think about, either. How do you wrap your mind around the fact that your woman was in trouble and there wasn't shit you could do about it? Nah, I wasn't going for that.

My face tightened as the muscles in my jaw flexed. I had spent the last thirty minutes combing the streets for Ox. Now, pulling up to Cam and Abe's crib, I felt the little piece of control I was hanging on to beginning to disappear. Somebody needed to get to making sense of this shit before bodies began to drop.

"Yo', Ox. What the fuck is going on?" I yelled into the phone, pressing it deeper to my ear. She didn't answer, and for the first time since I was a child, I experienced a feeling so foreign it took my breath away... fear. I wasn't scared of no man. But, losing Ox? That terror sprinkled fear all through my veins. She was my oxygen. How was I supposed to breathe without her?

"Ox!" I shouted again. "Don't do me like this. Call me. Say something, man." I heard myself begging. It was like, I was having an outer body experience. Everything was happening in slow motion. I saw myself walking into the house, I made my way into the basement where my old room was, and moved the floor board for my two pistols. Somebody was about to talk.

My fist landed through the wall as I let out a frustrated howl. "Fuck!"

"Dre, what the fuck, bro?" Camden made his way to the bottom of the steps. His forehead was creased as he took me in, waiting for an explanation for the big ass hole my fist had created in the wall.

My head was so clouded that I couldn't explain the situation if I tried. Instead, I snatched up my car keys and headed for the door with murder flowing through my veins. I needed to see blood. I felt the angel of death lurking around me as the tip of my fingers tingled. It had been a long time since I slipped into the darkness. Everybody thought I was this crazy, wild ass nigga. But, truth was, I was sane as fuck. I kept to myself, got paper, and loved on my people. There were certain things I didn't play about, though. My family and my paper. I loved both of them and I'd kill a whole village behind them both, too.

"Dre," Cam called after me, snapping me back to reality. I had zoned out for a second. I never turned to face him as I cocked my nine and kept trudging toward the door. If he didn't get it before, I could tell by the look that crept on Cam's face now, he understood it was a shoot first, ask questions later situation.

Cam had been down for me since the sandbox. We got into a lot of shit together and he'd proven to be as solid as solid could get. Blood couldn't make us tighter, which is why he knew me like the back of his hand. He knew that shit was about to get heavy, and I knew that was why he let out a frustrated sigh.

"Let me grab my shit, bro. Calm down." He ran his hand through his waves, then he took off for his room. I didn't stop to wait for him, knowing he'd meet me in the car. Every second counted. I had to find my rib.

Cam caught up to me just as I hopped inside my Maserati and started the engine. The tires screeched as I skidded off, speeding up the street. I didn't even know where to start looking for Ox. My body was moving off pure emotion, adrenaline and revenge. I had to calm down because I wasn't thinking straight and at the rate I was moving, I was going to fuck around and do something stupid. My nerves were shaky. I needed a blunt of that good shit... or a stiff drink. Ox was missing? Somebody snatched up my baby? Fuck!

I hit Ox's line a few more times before I shoved my fist into the steering wheel. This was damn near killing me. The thought of living without my rib took my breath away.

"Yo' Dre, you gon' have to tell me something. What's going on, man?" Cam asked, bracing himself on the dash. I was pushing ninety miles per hour in a forty-five, weaving in and out of traffic. I felt him staring intensely at me and I let out a sigh.

"Ox went and picked up the bag from Rah and somebody snatched her up." I finally whispered. Saying it out loud made it real. I felt my insides turn as I continued, "bro, you know I'm over here sick. I was supposed to be her protector. So many people done fucked over her. She don't deserve this." I shook my head as I swallowed the lump in my throat. I wasn't no hoe ass nigga. I couldn't even remember the last time I shed a tear. But, this shit here had me about to break.

"How you know somebody got her? Who stupid enough to fuck with us?" Cam asked and I shrugged.

"I mean, we was talking. She was sounding all trippy. Then, I heard some nigga say, *didn't yo' daddy-*" my voice trailed off as it all clicked in. That bitch ass nigga Doug finally grew some balls. I swear, it was a wrap for that nigga. His time had just expired.

He should have been dealt with a long time ago, but I spared him off the strength of Ox. Now, his pass had been revoked and if Ox had a scratch on her, he was going down as having the illest death in history. I was going to torture his bitch ass, slow, painful, and brutally.

I whipped my car around, making U-turn on Jefferson Ave. I knew I was on some reckless shit. Tires screeched. Horns blew. I didn't give a fuck, though. All types of sick shit flowed through my head. Shit that wouldn't even cross a normal person's mind.

"Wait, a minute, nigga. Slow this ma'fucka down before the hook get on us. We ridin' dirty as fuck right now." Cam barked. His body had slammed against the passenger door. That was how hard I turned the wheel. "Where you going?" He added.

"Bro, I don't want to talk right now. If you ridin', just ride." I turned the volume up on my speakers. The sound of Sada Baby pumped through the stereo, as the base caused the car to vibrate. I didn't mean to snap at Cam. But, I wasn't trying to hear that peacemaker, voice of reason bullshit.

There wasn't no reasoning.

***

"That ma'fucka gon' get his. I promise, Ox. I got you, ma." I whispered as my car crept to a slow stop three houses down from Doug's house. The sun had just begun to go down and the block was void of the regular hustle and bustle. I watched as Big Homie stood on his porch kicking it with that snake-ass, crack head bitch, Sherry. I felt the veins in my neck bulge. I tried my best to calm the urge to hop out the whip, spraying the block. I knew had to play it smart.

Cam tapped me, pointing to the porch. "There that nigga go right there. I doubt he got Ox, bro."

I ignored the nigga. Like I said before, there wasn't no reasoning. I pushed my door open and hopped out, with my eyes set on bitch-ass Doug. My trigger finger began to itch. But, I knew I couldn't burn the nigga until he told me where Ox was.

"Nephewww!" Sherry's snaggle-toothed ass squealed, announcing my presence. "Where you been?" She asked, extending her arms for a hug. Bitch had me fucked up and she knew it. Or, maybe it was the fire in my gaze as Doug and I locked eyes that had her dropping her arms and backing away. "Let me go. I'll call you later Dougie. Bye nephew." She was stumbling over her feet as she nearly ran off the porch.

Doug cockily smirked at me. "Lil' Dre, what the fuck you doing this way? You came to get ya' job back, lil' nigga? Finally realized a bitch can,"

My nine slammed against his dome, cutting his sentence short. I clocked him twice more before his shoulders slumped and his hand pressed against the side of his head. "Where the fuck Ox at?" I growled through tight lips.

"Nigga, have you lost your fu,"

Bam!

My nine slammed into his head again. This time, he stumbled as crimson-tinted liquid trickled from his forehead. I snatched him up by the collar, slamming him into the wall with my nine pressed to his dome. "Where… the fuck… is Ox?" I gritted.

"She ain't in my back pocket." He spat, attempting to snatch away. "Lil' nigga, if you don't plan to use that ma'fuckin gun, you better get that shit out my face."

Leave it to Doug to want to be tough with a barrel pointing at his temple. I let out a small laugh. Then, I snapped. Everything went black and the only thing I was focused on was seeing blood. I hated his bitch ass and even if he didn't have Ox, his slick ass mouth was reason enough to take him out the game.

"Broo! Niggas is watching you. This ain't how you handle it. How the fuck he gone tell you where Ox is if you kill him? We got to tell the crew, put everybody's heads together. We'll find her." Cam tried reasoning as he pulled me away from Doug.

The mention of Ox's name snapped me back to reality. Doug was crouched down, covering his bloody face. His bitch ass was tough when it came to beating on females and lil' niggas. But, he knew who to try that shit on. I sent my foot to his head one last time. "I know you sent yo' people to snatch up Ox. If you don't tell me where the fuck she at, I'm gon' start cutting off yo' fingers one by one. Then, I'm gon' take the hammer and knock your grill out, carve my name into ya' punk ass chest, and pour salt in all ya' wounds. Play with me Doug and you gon' wish I killed you the last time I beat ya' ass."

Doug let out a groan as he dropped to his knees. His white t-shirt was drenched in blood and his head was leaking. "I don't got her. This shit unnecessary, man. You gon' bite the hand that fed you, twice?" He finally muttered. "I didn't send nobody to do shit." The tough guy act was gone, but I wasn't convinced. I heard the nigga on the phone loud and clear.

I pressed my nine to his temple again. This time, if he didn't tell me what I wanted to here, I was burning him. "I said, where the fuck is Ox?" My tone was low and deadly. Revenge. Murder. Death.

"I ain't got her. What the fuck? I been letting y'all eat. Nigga, I fell back. The fuck I'm gon' get at y'all now for?" Now he wanted to cop pleas.

"Yeah, Dre. Chill man. The whole block out here watching. It ain't the time for that. You can't help Ox behind bars. We can holla at him later."

I squeezed the handle of the gun tighter. I wanted to end him tonight, but I knew Cam was right. Doug didn't have Ox and now wasn't the time to settle his debt. Cam had just gave him a couple of extra days to breathe. I knew that tonight ignited a war. Doug was old school. I should have used the pistol since I pulled it out. But, I was going to handle him as soon as I found Ox.

Chapter Three

Abe

I wasn't trying to fall in love. But, shit. The way Yonni rode my dick slow and real nasty-like with her eyes closed tight and a steady rhythm, I was ready to give her the code to the safe, my last name, and a few babies.

I shook my head, attempting to take my mind off of how good it felt. After the first time I fucked and busted prematurely, I had shit to prove. I was breaking her back every time I slid up in it.

I grabbed her hips to slow her down. "Damn, girl. Why you tryin' to have a nigga on some sucka shit?" I groaned, smacking her fat cheeks.

Yonni had an onion ass that was fat enough to make a grown man cry. Lil' momma was thick to death and sexy as fuck. She wasn't like these other broads. Usually, I could hit and be on my way without a second thought. She had me spending time with her, going on dates, and caking on the phone. I saw myself slowly changing and I didn't like that shit. There was too much pussy in the world to be trapped with one chick.

"You better not cum, lil' nuts. Take this pussy baby," She teased and all I could do was shake my head at her crazy ass. She was trying to play me like a sucka; like I wouldn't demolish her lil' coochie and have her walking bowlegged for the next few weeks.

Catching her off guard, I flipped her on her back and slid in her deep and hard, missionary style. "Nah, you take this dick," I growled. "Fuck you mean."

She giggled biting down on her bottom lip. Her sparkling hazels were trying to stare into my soul. That shit was too deep for me. So, I turned her onto her stomach and propped her ass up, hitting it from the back. "You gon' stop fuckin' wit' me, girl. You gon' learn who the fuckin' king is," I grunted. Her tight walls were sucking me in like a hoover vacuum and squeezing my joint like a glove.

"We both know what it is. Whose dick is this, Abraham?" She taunted. "That's right, take momma's pussy."

I couldn't help laughing at her. She was a straight character. She loved testing me to my limit. Yonni knew I'd act a fool up in that pussy and that's exactly what she wanted me to do.

"You... don't... run... shit!" I growled, going deep and hard. I was trying to hit her esophagus with each stroke. The harder I went, the tighter her pussy became. She loved that rough sex.

"Yes, Abraham. Harder!" She demanded. I gave her exactly what she wanted, hard-stroking her until her muscles began to contract and we both exploded together.

Rolling off of her, I fell onto my back, exhausted. I didn't even feel like taking the condom off. Sex with Yonni was never regular. That shit was off the chain and intense, had a nigga spent.

Yonni turned to me, a smile spread across her almond face. She was gorgeous. That was something I could never deny. "Do you love me Abraham?"

"What?" I frowned. That question was random as hell.

"Do you love me? You heard me. We've been kicking it for months and I don't know what it is. This is getting deep and I need to know what's up so I can play things accordingly. I'm not about to be loyal pussy to a nigga that's not trying to appreciate it."

Here she goes with the bullshit. Did I love Yonni? I didn't know about all that. I cared for her more than any other broad. I liked kicking it, but that love shit was for the birds.

I sighed, turning over on my back. "Why you trying to make shit complicated. Why you can't just enjoy this dick?"

"Because I can get a wet ass from anywhere. I'm not about to waste my time and energy on meaningless fucks. For the first time in a long time, I'm doing what I want. I fell out with my own mother fucking with you. So, of course I want to know if it's worth it."

"So, that's what this about, huh? You using me to prove a point to yo' old bird? Don't try to change me into a nigga that I ain't because you can't stand up to yo' momma."

Yonni rolled her pretty eyes. "Sometimes, I think you're really clueless, Abraham. In case you haven't paid attention, I'm not these ditzy hoes. I don't need to use you for nothing. I'm spending time with you because I genuinely like you. But, don't get it twisted, I have no problem moving along and acting like you never existed."

Yonni was on a nigga hard. As much as she tried to play it off like she was still in control, I knew she was really in her feelings. I was too. This whole situation was new to me. Yonni was the closest thing I ever had to a girlfriend and I wasn't ready to commit.

Instead of responding, I grabbed my cell from off the nightstand. I had a total of twenty-two missed calls and fifteen texts from the crew. I even had a call from Yonni's worrisome ass mother. Cherish never liked me and I couldn't stand her ass either, so I knew something serious had to have went down. Our phones had been on silent since the night before and the only time we came back to reality was to rest and use the bathroom.

I dialed Dre back first and when he didn't answer, I hit Cam's line. He picked up on the second ring. "Damn, nigga. You finally decided to answer your phone?" Cam blasted.

I frowned. "What's up, bro? I ain't hear the ma'fucka ringing."

"They hit us. Got the bag and Ox. Shit been crazy for the past few hours."

"Damn, that's fucked up. Did Ox see who did it?"

Cam blew out a breath of air. "Didn't you just hear me say somebody got Ox? They snatched her. We don't know shit. So why you playing house, get yo' shit and you and Yonni meet us at Deek's crib. Cherish flew in and we got a meeting."

The line went dead and all I could do was stare at the phone. I was slipping. Today was the day I was supposed to pick up the drop. But, I said fuck it, messing around with Yonni. Fuck! Now somebody had Ox and I knew everything was about to come down on me.

"We got to go," I told Yonni, never giving her an explanation. I hopped up and began to throw my shit in my duffle bag.

"What's going on Abraham? You're scaring me." Yonni hopped up too.

"Somebody snatched up Ox." I shook my head, pacing the floor. "Here I am playing with you and shit all bad. They done got my nigga Ox."

Reality began to settle in. The streets of Detroit were cold. Niggas got murdered and came of missing everyday. I didn't want that for Ox. She didn't deserve it. Just the thought of what she was going through had me rushing toward the door.

"Oh, God. Let's go Abraham. Hurry up." Yonni yelled, two steps ahead of me. "Please don't let nothing happen to my sister. Please!"

After grabbing our things, we hopped in my truck doing ninety on the dash all the way to Rahdeek's house. All I could think about was Ox. I knew Dre was going nuts. They had this weird ass deep connection that only they understood, but I felt it.

Yonni had her phone pressed to her ear the whole ride over. I could tell that she was talking to Cherish. It was like, when she got into the outside world, she was a lioness. But, when it came to her mother, she lost her roar.

A single tear fell down her left cheek. I wanted to wipe it away. But she did it herself so fast that I wouldn't have believed she shed a tear if I hadn't seen it with my own two eyes. The fact that seeing her cry affected me had me in my feelings. I was trying so hard not to care, but deep down, I did.

Reaching over to grab her had, I squeezed it. "You know you too hard to be crying, right? Whatever the case is, remember you're a grown ass woman, aight? Stop letting your mother dictate your life."

"My mother is my best friend, Abraham. I don't have a problem with her."

"You do. But, you ain't admitting it. You still want to be that child in her eyes. You need to spread your wings and be the beast you be trying to bully me with."

She giggled and I smiled too. "I don't bully you, Abraham."

"Shiiit. You be running up on a nigga and strong arming him."

"Whatever. I don't want to laugh right now. My sister is missing. My mother just cursed me out and-"

"You forgot to add you just had the best dick of your life." I teased, causing her to laugh again.

"Abraham! I'm serious. My mother is pissed."

"What's new?" I shrugged. "I don't be thinkin' about that lady. What she say about Ox?"

"That we better find her. The ball was dropped and she's blaming everyone. Apparently, Rah gave Ox the bag that you were supposed to pick up and someone robbed and kidnapped her."

"So how is that everybody's fault? Her nigga fucked up. If I wasn't there, he was supposed to call Dre or Cam. He wasn't supposed to give shit to Ox."

"You care about what we have going on, right? I mean, put your pride to the side before answering."

"We kicking it. Where that come from?"

"Because she's going to try to keep us apart and I know what I feel. So, I want to make sure that you strap your nuts on Lil' Nuts."

I stared at Yonni. I felt that foreign feeling that crept in my chest every time she smiled at me. She was going to be a problem. Yon was dangerous to my heart. I knew that leaving her alone was the best thing to do in order to keep business straight. But, I also knew when it came to Deyonni, I wasn't about to let her look crazy in front of her old bird. If she wanted to stand up to Cherish, I'd be on my worst asshole behavior. I had her back.

Chapter Four

Cam

Rahdeek stayed in a condo off the river in downtown Detroit. It was less than five minutes from Ox and Dre's crib, but I couldn't get this nigga Dre off the couch for shit. We had combed the streets, him terrorizing the city, me trying to calm him the fuck down. Yet, six hours later, there still wasn't any sign of Ox.

I watched as he tossed back his fifth shot of Hennessy. A scowl was plastered across his face and his eyes were set low. I sighed. "Come on, bro. Cherish wants us to meet her at Rah's crib." I tried urging him to get up.

"Fuck Cherish," Dre grumbled, waving me off. I wasn't used to seeing him vulnerable. Dre was a tough ass nigga, and he never showed emotions. If it wasn't for the way he loved Ox, I would have been convinced he didn't have a soul. So, I understood why he was going nuts over Ox being missing.

I shook my head. "Nah, bro. It ain't fuck her. She ain't did shit to us. Fuck sitting around moping. That's not going to bring Ox back. They got their ears to the streets. Let's see what they talking about."

Dre's eyes slanted toward me. "All this shit Deek's fault. Why the fuck would he give Ox the bag, bro? Every time I think about that stupid shit, I want to put a bullet to his dome." He paused for a second, staggering to his feet. “As a matter of fact, let’s go. We need to see his bitch ass.”

I shook my head, following him toward the door, pushing it closed as he opened it. “Nah, man. You know Ox was out of line too. We had a process. She shouldn’t have picked up the bag alone. But, this ain’t the blame game. We need to focus on getting her back.”

Dre held himself up on the wall. He was beyond drunk. “You right, nigga.” His neck slowly craned up toward me. “But what am I supposed to do? I can’t just keep dropping bodies with no results. But on some real shit, I’ll murder this whole fucking city. How I’m supposed to breathe without my lungs? That ma'fucka my whole lifeline.”

Damn, I felt bad for both Ox and Dre. We had to find her. We had to get things back to normal.

***

An hour later, everything was all bad. We had made it to Rah's condo, but adrenaline was at an all time high. Everyone was reacting off emotions and no one was trying to be logical about the shit.

We walked in to Cherish going off on Abe. Man, why she smack this nigga so hard that the sound echoed throughout the entire room. I knew it took everything in Abe not to knock her ass out. I saw it in his face that he wanted to.

Dre didn’t make the situation any better. As soon as he saw Rahdeek, he went at him. They got to arguing and now here we were trying to break up a pissing match between two crazy ass niggas. Dre was off his rocker, but Rahdeek was one of those silent crazy niggas. You never saw him coming until the hot lead was exploding your dome.

"You real tough right now, youngin'. And I feel you. But this ain't for us. I'm sure you know I ain't the nigga to play with."

Dre's chest puffed. He had that look in his eye. I'd known him long enough to know when he was about to do something crazy. So, I stepped in front of him. No matter what the situation was, Rah and Cherish were the plug. We may have gotten close, but they weren't no peons. Going to war with our own crew when we were already fighting an outside battle was the last thing we needed.

"Chill, Dre." I warned, tapping his shoulder. He and Deek were locked in a deep stare down, both men throwing I-don't-give-a-fuck vibes.

"The fuck I got to chill for? This nigga right here lookin' like he want to do something. What you want to do, nigga?" Dre growled.

I had to shake my head. "Come on y'all. Now ain't the time to be falling apart." I warned. "Come on, bro. Walk it off. They here to help, Dre." I wasn't getting through to this nigga. He had murder in his eyes, knocking on Deek's door. I knew that Rah wasn't afraid to answer too.

"Fuck that. You got a problem Rah?" Dre tried stepping around me. "I thought we was good. I looked up to you, nigga. And you gon' do some hoe ass shit like that to Ox? Set her ass up for failure."

Obviously Deek was done talking. His tall frame began to disappear down the hallway. "I ain't got time for this shit," He muttered.

"This is unacceptable. How could y'all not protect the queen? I knew I gave y'all entirely too much power." Cherish ran her hand through her hair, pacing. "I don't give a damn what needs to be done. Find Oxtavia and the niggas that's responsible. I would say bring them to me, but I'm sure DeAndre has the punishment under control. The blocks will be shut down until further notice."

"What?" Abe frowned. "What sense does that make? Why stop the money?"

Cherish ran her tongue over her teeth. "I advice you not to talk to me. It's taking everything in me not to harm you. I told you to leave my daughter alone and not only did you not obey me, you allowed us to get hit while sitting around playing house with her."

"Nah, if your slow ass nigga didn't give her the drop, she would be good. Don't make this a me thing because you trying to control her pussy."

Cherish stepped into Abe's face. Her long hair was pulled back into a ponytail and the jogging suit was unusual for her classy swag. "You know why I don't want you with my daughter? Because she's too good for your stupid ass. You still want to be seen. You're still into childish bullshit. You're not capable of being a man." She stepped so close to Abe that their noses were almost touching. "And I'm a different kind of parent. Before I see my child hurt, I'll chop your motherfucking head off. We do business together, Abraham. I'm trying to keep it professional. But don't make me fall out with everyone because you want some pussy."

"Ma!" Yonni shrieked. "I know what I'm doing. You don't have to worry about that."

Cherish smirked. "I'm not worried. Meeting's adjourned. Please hit the streets and find something out about Oxtavia."

Cherish's hips swayed as she walked off, joining Rahdeek in the back. I watched as everything happened. I saw the operation beginning to unravel and I also knew that I needed to start making my exit plan. This shit was about to fall apart.

***

After dropping Dre back off to his house, I made my way to Kelsey's house. She stayed in a nice apartment building out in Southfield. I hadn't seen her since she called herself walking out on me at the house party. I didn't even know if she was at home. All I knew was that I needed her. Kelsey was my peace. She took me away from the reality of my world and showed me there was more out there. I appreciated her for that shit.

"What are you doing here, Camden?" Kelsey's almond tinted face crinkled as she took me in, standing there in front of her doorsteps lost as fuck. Kelsey was the epitome of beautiful. She had this innocent, genuine glow about her that was sexy as hell and she was thick to death. Not that build-a-body thickness. She was naturally round and curvaceous.

I shrugged shoving my hands in my pockets. "So, I can't come see my queen now? I missed you, Kels."

She bit down on her bottom lip as her messy ponytail flopped in her face. "I don't want to do this if you're still in the streets or still have that girl in your face. I want peace, Ca-"

"Shut up," I cut her off, stepping into her face. "Fuck what you talking about. I miss you girl. I need you Kels. Everything is all bad and you're the only peace I got right now."

She stepped to the side for me to walk into her apartment. Then, she locked the door and turned to say something. But, I cut her off, crushing my lips into hers. "I just want to hear that you got my back. Do you got me?" I asked, as my finger traced her hard nipple and my lips found their way to the crook of her neck. "Tell me you got me, Kels."

She nodded, letting out a moan. "You know I do, Camden. I just want better for the both of us."

"We gon' get it." I assured her, using my chest to guide us toward her bedroom as my hands explored her curves. She was rocking this thin ass tank top and booty shorts. My soldier was at full salute, ready to break her back.

"Promise?"

"I put that on our future. I got you. Just let me have you. Can I do that?" I asked, pulling down her shorts as we made it to her room. Her caramel legs were silky and her pussy was bald. That mafucka was talking to me.

Kelsey's mouth fell open to speak, but as I tossed her onto the bed and climbed between her legs, no words came out. Her pretty pussy was in my face and that ma'fucka was calling out to me, smelling like fresh flowers and *her*.

My lips traced the inside of her thigh, trailing to her southern lips until I found the spot I was looking for. I took her clit into my mouth, playing with it;

licking, nibbling, and kissing it. I saw her body tense with anticipation. She was squirming, anxious for me to tongue kiss her pearl properly.

I took her out of her misery, sucking on her clit like it was my last meal. Her pussy's taste was just for me. The way she began to moan sounded so sweet. Fuck, this girl had me open. I'd give her the world if I could.

"Shit, Camden." She growled with her eyes closed tightly.

"Camden what? Look at me Kelsey. Tell me how you want me to kiss yo' pussy." I whispered into her sweetness as my eyes stood trained on her face. "Like this?" I asked whirling my tongue around the perimeter of her clit. She jumped. "Or like this?" I mumbled, clamping down hard and sucking.

"Ahhh, Camden! Like that baby." She squealed.

I watched her pleasure faces and just when I was sure she was about to nut, I flipped her on her back and slid inside of her deep and hard, gaining full access to her heaven on earth.

"Damn, Kels. I think I love you, girl. Tell me this my pussy. Tell me you got me through whatever." I groaned, slow stroking her sweet walls. I wasn't fucking tonight. I was making love to my woman. In the world of chaos that I had just been thrown into, I needed to feel love... I needed to feel my woman.

Chapter Five

Ox

His tall frame stalked over to me. I felt the devil lurking, I saw it in his eyes. He no longer had a mask on, which meant they didn't care anymore. I hated when they left me alone with him. It seemed as if beating me got his dick hard.

"I'm tired of playing these games with you, bitch. You need to take us to the money." The dude I learned name was CJ paced the floor right above my head.

I had been tied to a chair in the basement for the past two days. My entire body ached from being beaten, my clothes were dirty, and my throat was dry. I didn't even respond because I didn't have the strength to.

I couldn't take them to the stash house because I knew that only one person would be there, which meant they could easily get the money and kill me because they wouldn't need me anymore. I wished that I could somehow talk to Dre.

I felt my hair being ripped out of my scalp as my head jerked upward. "You here me talking to you bitch? Where the fucking money at?" He seethed through clenched teeth.

"It's locked away. I can't get to it." I whispered, feeling as my head began to throb. He knocked me in it and began to snap. He used his fists, hands, and feet to punish me and in this very moment, I wished that he would just kill me already. The pain was unbearable.

I heard the front door open and footsteps cascade down the basement steps. I could barely see who it was, though. CJ had hit me so hard in the face that both of my eyes barely opened.

"Yo', what the fuck you doing nigga?" That was Sunny. I had learned his voice because he was my savior. Whenever the beatings got too intense, he would be the one to step in to stop them. Sometimes, he wouldn't allow them to touch me at all. "Didn't I say that's not how we're carrying things?" He growled, pushing CJ back.

"Man, fuck this broad. I'm tired of playing with her." I didn't recognize that voice. It was new. "Have this nigga kick a bone out her ass, get the dough, and ditch her. We got other licks to hit. We done wasted two days on this broad."

Sunny sighed. "We wasn't supposed to waste no days. All we had to do was grab the bag and be on to the next lick. Now we got a situation that I ain't got time for." He was mad. I heard the frustration in his voice.

"With yo' peacemaker ass," The new voice chuckled. I heard his footsteps as he neared me. My body tensed. I hadn't been this scared or helpless ever in life. What my father did to me was nothing compared to the torture they were putting me through. At least I knew my father wouldn't kill me; however, with them, my life was dangling in their hands.

"Fuck," a shoe came crashing to my stomach. "This," a blow hit my neck. "Bitch," I couldn't comprehend where the last blow hit because everything went black. I was definitely going to die.

***

“Yo’, wake up.” I felt the light taps on my cheeks but I was still too dazed to comprehend it. “Get up and eat something.”

Sunny. That was definitely Sunny trying to feed me. But, I didn’t want nothing from him unless he was trying to let me leave. I hated him and everyone involved in kidnapping me… all over a couple of dollars.

I should have never gone to pick up the money. I cursed myself out a thousand times, thinking of how I could have done things differently. I should have listened.

“Man, I don’t really give a fuck if you eat or not. It don’t make me no difference. You stubborn as fuck when all you have to do is give up the bag and get this fuck shit over with.”

“It won’t be over with. Y’all are going to kill me.” I whispered, feeling the rumbling in my stomach. The food smelled good. I couldn’t remember the last time I had eaten.

“If I was going to let them kill you, you would have been dead baby girl. I ain’t no killer. I take nigga’s shit. All I want is the money. But you ain’t helping me to help you.”

My mind was going a mile a minute. Sunny was in charge. I figured that out the first night they snatched me. But, whoever the Man nigga was, he was in charge too and they were playing tug of war with the power. If I could convince Sunny to let me go, I knew he would be my best bet for survival. He wasn’t like them.

“What is that?” I finally gave in. “It smells good.”

"Steak bites from Starters. I went and got me something, so I grabbed you something too."

I frowned. "How am I supposed to eat with my hands tied up?"

Sunny let out a sigh. "You got to figure that shit out."

"But how? What can I do if you untie my hands? I can barely move from y'all beating me so bad."

"Nah, I ain't touched you. It's yo' fault though. Why the fuck you so stubborn, man? Tell us where the bag is and lets get this shit over with."

I looked off, as he began to untie my wrists. My first thought was to kick him in the balls and run. But, I knew I wouldn't get far. I needed Sunny on my side.

"Can I make a phone call. Just to let everybody know I'm okay. I mean, how much money do y'all want? I can get Dre to just bring it to you."

Sunny chuckled. "Nice try. You not about to set me up for failure and have them niggas busting down my door."

I rolled my eyes. "How? I don't even know where I'm at, Sunny."

He frowned. "Yo', don't be saying my name like you know me. Names will get you popped with the quickness."

"I don't give a damn about knowing anyone else's name. I know you're the one that calls the shots. You hold my life in your hands. And..." I paused, laying it on thick. "I know that you have a heart. I wouldn't play you. I just don't want them to give up hope. Please let me call DeAndre. Just to hear my voice."

There was a long pregnant pause, before Sunny stood and left out the room. I thought I fucked everything up until he returned with a cheap ass burner phone. I knew it had to be one because it was so outdated.

"What's the number?"

I read off Dre's number trying not to sound too anxious. But I was ecstatic. This was my one shot. I couldn't blow it.

Before passing me the phone, Sunny's deep brown eyes fastened on me. "Look, don't be on no bullshit. I've been the only nigga lookin' out through this fucked up situation. Aight?"

I nodded, ignoring the ringing pain with the shake of my head. "I promise."

He passed me the phone and I felt my adrenaline rush as it rung. "Who the fuck is this?" It was Dre. Hearing his voice sent a chill up my spine and rushed to my head.

"Baby, I need you." I felt the tears as they seeped from my eyes.

"Ox? Yo'! Where the fuck you at, ma?"

"I don't knowww. They got me. CJ and Man. Help-" Before I could finish, Sunny snatched the phone, hanging it up. All bets were off. I poured my soul out to my man and if I died in the process, I hoped he found them.

“The fuck is you doing?” Sunny growled. “I call myself helping you and this what you do? Bet!” He paced the floor.

“I didn’t mention your name. And quite frankly, I think you want to be done with them anyways, but you in too deep.”

“You don’t know shit!” Sunny roared. He knocked a rack over, before storming over to me and re-tying my wrists. “A nigga can’t even help your retarted ass. You must want to die.”

I didn’t say a word. I was content. I heard my baby’s voice. I gave him the names of our enemies. I knew that it would only be a matter of time before he found me... hopefully my time wouldn’t run out before he did.

***

Sunny

I listened to ol' girl as she tossed and turned, uncomfortable. She had went through the same routine every night since she made it to my house. I felt bad for her. These niggas were on some extra shit. I was all for getting to the bag, but I wasn’t with beating on the broad and violating her the way CJ had been doing.

I released a breath of air, as I finally decided that I was over hearing her whimper. I wanted my peace back, but I was scared to let them sick ass niggas take her out of my protection until I figured out what I wanted to do with her. Manny acted like he wanted her dead and CJ just didn’t give a fuck.

When I linked with Man and his people, it was all about snatching the bag and getting the fuck on. I was a simple nigga. I didn’t do all the hot shit. I stayed to myself and got my paper up. I knew it was time to separate myself from them dumb niggas. They were reckless.

Growing frustrated, I decided to hit the streets and clear my head. I shouldn't have given a fuck. But, I did. Lil' Momma reminded me of my sister. Raynesha was murdered when she was seventeen by some big time dope boy that liked fucking little girls. We all tried to warn her but, she got in over her head. He did sis dirty, left her naked and beaten body in a city trashcan. The . I would never forget the day we got that phone call. We hadn't been the same since.

I didn't want to think of those thoughts. Man knew the deal and he still brought this shit around me. I shook my head as I called up this little chick named Shabon that I had been dealing with.

"Oh, you finally got time for me, huh? You're so full of shit, Sunny." She boomed into the phone.

I thought I was going to get some pussy to relieve some stress, but I didn't have time for the mouth, so I decided to grab a pint of Cîroc and head back to the crib.

I stopped by the store in the hood, parking right at the door. It was just past midnight and the parking lot was empty with the exception of a Range Rover. I walked into the store and almost froze with shock. I wasn't no hoe ass nigga, but I wasn't expecting to see ol' girl's boyfriend. I remembered him from the hood, but I don't think he remembered me.

We stared at each other. I could see the anguish in his face. I knew it all too well. When my sister came up missing, I felt like I lost my soul.

“The fuck you lookin' at nigga. Got a problem?” He growled.

I smirked, looking away. He didn’t even know who the fuck I was, I had the key to his future laying in my front room... I just had to decide what I wanted to do with her.

Chapter Six

Dre

She was alive. Hearing Ox's voice had the tightening is my chest loosening just a little. I wasn't going to be all the way right until she was back by my side, though. Whoever snatched her was going to get it the worst way possible. I put that on my unborn kids.

I punched the steering wheel as I rode up Dexter Ave. Taking a pull from the blunt I had been smoking, I released a thick cloud into the air. I had smoked four blunts in the past hour and nothing was getting me high enough to make sense of everything. I didn't know who was brazen enough to snatch up Ox. When she screamed Man and CJ's name, that shit had me boggled. They couldn't have been from the hood, and they didn't make any demands. They just hung up. Now, my head was all messed up because I didn't know what they wanted from us.

I thought about talking to God, maybe asking him to help. But, that nigga had never done nothing for me. If he cared, he really had a fucked up way of showing it. I guess I had done so much foul shit that he didn't have time for a nigga like me.

I was lost. Ox was the only human being other than my mom that I allowed to penetrate my mental and control my peace. She was all that I had. I swear, I wasn't sane without Ox by my side and I'd die if she left me. Our souls had mated. She was the poison that ran through my veins and she was also the anecdote that kept them pumping.

I found myself sitting in front of my old bird's crib on Chicago. The Salvation Army across the street was throwing some kind of function. Kids were running up the block and adults were chilling in lawn chairs. I searched for my mother. If she was sober, she would have been out there enjoying the festivities. So, when I didn't find her, I knew she had to be still on her shit. I didn't have time to be dealing with her bullshit and Ox too. I started to pull off, but a nigga needed his mother. I'd take her in any capacity.

Sometimes I resented Ronnie. She put me through hell growing up the son of a crackhead. I didn't get the normal childhood like everyone else. She was on that shit and poor. So, I had to rob, steal, and kill to survive.

I swallowed those ill thoughts, pushing my way through the doors of my mother's apartment. The smell of old wood, piss, and a fresh cooked meal immediately hit my nostrils. However, when I made it through my mother's door, I was taken completely by surprise. He place smelled like fresh pine, Karen White was singing in the background, and I found my mother in the kitchen slaving over a stove. Ronnie was sober.

I had to be tough too long. I was tired of being tough. That's why the sight of my mother the way I remembered her before . shit took control of her caused me to break.

"Dre?" Her face crinkled with concern. "I didn't even hear you come in. I was going to call you and Oxy to get a pl-" She paused, making her way over to me and wrapping her frail arms around me. "You're about to scare me, DeAndre. I'm not strong enough for this shit. You're crying. What happened." She whispered.

A mother's love was a motherfucker. I couldn't remember the last time Ronnie wrapped her arms around me in a nurturing way. All the pain I had bottled up came pouring out. This shit should have been given to every child freely. I fought for my mother to love me enough to get straight. I killed for her to realize how much her addiction affected me. I was really fucked up in the head. But, having my mother finally rub my back and tell me everything would be okay with a sober tongue temporarily relieved the caked of tension in my chest.

"Dre, please tell me what's wrong. You're my strength. I need you to be strong for me. Where's Oxy? Shit. I need a cigarette."

"Somebody got her." I shrugged, pulling myself together. I wasn't no soft ass nigga. "I been trying to find her a night. It's been damn near twenty-four hours and still no signs of Ox." I shook my head. "I'm fucked up. I was supposed to protect her and I didn't."

"You always put the weight of the world on your shoulders, Dre Dre." My mother sighed. "Ox is going to be okay. We're not claiming nothing else. God go-"

I pushed out of her arms, shaking my head. "No disrespect," I cut her off. "But, I don't want to talk about that nigga. Where was he when everything was fucked up eighty percent of my life? Then, when I get a little piece of peace, he come snatching that shit away? I'm sorry ma, but I'm not feeling that nigga right now."

"You can't blame God for your life being messed up. He didn't make me hit that pipe. He didn't push you into the streets. We get it fucked up because we want to do things our own way instead of his way. Well, I'm tired of doing it my way, DeAndre. Look at me. I been sober a whole week and the taste of crack ain't been on my tongue once. That's God."

I shook my head, over the preachy shit. "Man, whatever. For how long? Things been messed up so long, I can't even be happy for your sobriety."

My mother's lips formed a pout. "Well, I'm happy for myself. Nothing is going to make me go back to the pipe and I know it's nobody but God. And, I also know that he's going to find Ox for you."

"Oh, yeah. So why now? All of a sudden you're delivered?"

She looked off, taking a step back, and shrugging. "Because I'm tired of being a crackhead."

My old bird said that shit as if it was easy as 1-2-3. So, she wasn't tired when I begged her to get clean for me growing up... or when I caught my first body behind her monkey shit. I was never good enough to get clean for, huh?

Everything was too much. I had to get away from her. I needed a blunt and my baby. I had to find Ox before I went completely crazy. Nothing would be right until she was back.

Chapter Seven

Abe

I needed some warm pussy and a blunt to relax my mind. Shit was crazy in the streets. We were in the middle of a war. For a week straight, we wreaked havoc; snatching niggas up, busting through spots, and pushing hot lead through nigga's domes. Ox was still missing and we weren't any closer to finding the nigga CJ or Man.

For a second, I was starting to think that Dre was hallucinating. He was breaking with each day that passed, getting more ruthless by the second. Whoever the fuck they were, they were tucked safely. Nobody knew who they were.

If we didn't find Ox soon, Dre was going to end up behind bars. I thought about the night before and shook my head. The way he beat that lil' nigga Cortez was fucked up. I knew he didn't even have shit to do with anything. He was just at the wrong place at the wrong time.

To make matters worse, Cherish had completely stopped our cash flow. She shut all the blocks down until we found Ox. I wasn't feeling that shit at all. We had customers that needed their shit and wouldn't be scared to jump ship. My pockets were used to pulling in a steady cash flow. I had been living it up, so I was starting to feel the pain. I loved Ox to death, like a sister, but I didn't see a need in shutting down business. We could run our operation and find Ox at the same time.

Between dealing with the kidnapping situation, the money slowing up, and Yonni's clingy ass, I was about to go crazy. I needed a mental break. So, I decided to chill with this fine little yellow bone I met a few months back. Her name was Lasonya. She had a mean little head game and she was cute in the face. Sonya was one of those bourgeois broads. I knew she was after the paper, but I also knew how to play her. All I wanted was to get my dick wet and take my head off the bullshit for a second.

However, an hour into our date, I was already ready to send her ass home in an Uber. She reminded me why I didn't court these bird brain broads. Yonni was making a nigga soft. Before her, I was a dog. I shook my head, trying to ignore the fact that I wished Deyonni was sitting across from me instead of Sonya.

As if she heard me thinking about her, a text came through from Yonni and I had to check myself as a smile plastered across my face reading it.

Yonni

Where you at Lil Nuts? I'm hungry.

She was always with the bullshit. She knew I hated when she called me Lil Nuts. I was a grown ass man with a big ass dick that cracked her back every time we fucked.

I quickly texted her back.

Me

With this fine ass chick, wishing it was you.
What you want to eat? I'm about to ditch this broad.

Yonni

You always playing with me like I'm not crazy.
Fuck you and that food.

I started to respond, but I wasn't trying to be sitting up arguing with that girl all night. She wasn't my lady. I was free to do whatever the fuck I wanted to do.

When I focused on Sonya, she was staring at me with her lips all tight. "What's wrong with you?" I frowned, stuffing my phone back in my pocket.

"You're disrespectful. You asked me out, but you're sitting across from me texting some other bitch."

I frowned. "Whooa, you don't know what I was doing, lil' momma. And for the record, I can do what the fuck I want to do. You ain't my woman. I ain't obligated to you."

Her brown eyes fluttered. "So, why did you call me here Abraham? I don't have time to be wasted. You got my number, had sex with me, and ignored me for two whole months. Do you think you can pop up when you please?"

I chuckled. "You know you had the option to say no, right? You the one that decided you wanted to fuck with me tonight."

"Whatever," She frowned, looking over the menu. We were at J. Alexander's out in Troy. "What made you even call me, Abraham? Is this how it's going to be going forward? You make time for me only when you want?"

I could have just took Yonni out for all this. "Man, I'm a busy nigga. My schedule cleared up for a minute. So, I'm trying to bless you with a little time and some dick." I smiled, taking her in. Sonya was bad ass hell. Maybe she was worth hitting it again then putting her on the block list.

"But, I'm here now. So what's up?"

"What's up is I'm not having sex with you. People make time for what they want. I have my shit together, Abraham. I'm definitely not ugly. I can get a man."

I frowned. "Well, we wasting each other's time. All I got is a little dinner and some dick." The waitress walked over to take our order, but I waved her off. "Nah, we need a few minutes. Come back in a few, beautiful." I watched as she walked off. She had a fat ass. I bet she would have been grateful sitting across from me. I focused on Sonya. "So, are we fucking or not?" I wasn't pressed for no pussy, and I definitely wasn't pressed to be in her presence. If I wanted to chill with a broad, I would have hit up Yonni. She got on my last nerve, but we could kick it. She kept a nigga on his toes.

Lasonya sighed. "No. Can we at least get to know each other, damn? Can we do more than lay me on my back?"

"Nope," I knew that voice from anywhere. "Because that's all the fuck you is to him. Both you and this nigga got me fucked up." Yonni stood in the front of our table, with her hands pressed to her thick hips, looking like a fucking goddess. I didn't know what it was about her but lil' momma was the toughest broad I ever met.

Wait, how the fuck did she find me? I shook my head, amused. I didn't know if I was turned on by the fact that she was claiming this dick, or annoyed by the way she ran up on me.

"Really, Abraham?" Sonya squeaked. "Who is she?"

Yonni's little button nose crinkled. "You don't even sound right calling him that. Call him Abe like the other basic bitches. As a matter of fact, don't call him at all." She sat down next to me, ignoring Sonya. "Keep playing with me Lil' Nuts." She warned, snatching the menu out of my hands and staring at it.

"Really?" Lasonya's head cocked. "I'm not about to sit here with you and her. Can you take me home, *Abraham*?"

Yonni crossed her arms over her chest. "I wish he would. You better click them last season ass heels and find your way back to wherever you came from."

I burst into laughter. "Man, you wildin'. Let me take this girl home and I'll meet you at the house."

"Hmph, I bet you won't." Yonni was stubborn as hell and I didn't care enough to fight with her. So, I sat there as we both looked over the menu. "What are you ordering?" Yonni asked as if Sonya wasn't sitting across from us.

"You know what," Sonya snatched her purse up. "Lose my number Abraham. I swear, I don't want to hear from you ever again." She stormed off, missing the fact that she was going on the block list as soon as I dropped her off anyway.

Yonni popped me in the chest as soon as Sonya disappeared. “So, I can’t even go to the mall without seeing you being disrespectful? My fucking sister is missing, I’m losing my mind, and you choose to entertain a basic bitch? You are so selfish. Sometimes, I wonder why I’m even trying with you.”

“Selfish?” My brows furrowed. “Last time I checked, I ain’t married. We kick it, but I can do whatever the fuck I want to do.” I was starting to feel like a broken record.

Yonni smiled. “Well, the way I see it, the minute you decided to fuck me, my pussy became the ring and your dick became the finger. Don’t play with me Abraham. Got this bitch calling you by your full government like she knows you.”

“You call me it,”

“Because I ain’t these other bitches!” Yonni screamed all up in these people’s restaurant.

I couldn’t stop laughing. She was really getting hot. “I know it. That’s why I let you irk my nerves. You in a league of your own, Yon.” I spoke facts. I knew that she was wife material… but I wasn’t ready to wife no broad.

She rolled her eyes. “Well, act like it then. Stop being scared of your feelings and come at me correctly, Abraham. We joke around a lot but I’m not one of these silly broads. Dick comes a dime a dozen for a woman like me. I don’t know what it is about you, but I like you. Stop having me looking stupid, Abraham.”

“You can never look stupid,”

"Whatever, you got me fucked up." She muttered, attempting to stand up, but I pulled her back down.

"Where you going? We might as well get something to eat and go back to the crib. You owe me some pussy since you fucked up my night."

"I wish I would," Yonni snarled, snatching away. "Never will I ever piggyback off the next broad's date and you definitely won't be getting any of this sweet pussy. I'm an emotional wreck because my sister is missing and this is how you play it? You better get acquainted with your hands tonight, Lil Nuts. Hopefully you wake up in the morning and realize who you're dealing with."

I let her leave. She didn't know who *she* was dealing with. I could call up another broad as soon as she walked out. But, I wasn't feeling the way she had me feeling some type of way. She needed to know that she wasn't running shit. If I pulled up on her tonight, she would definitely be getting her guts dug out.

Chapter Eight

Cam

Gazing at the cream paint of her sealing, I took a second to relax and get my head together. Kelsey and I had been kicking it tough ever since I popped up at her apartment. When I wasn't in the streets, we were kicking it, building and shit.

Kelsey had me reevaluating my entire life. We had been discussing business plans, talking about me going back to school to grab my G.E.D., and planning our future. I couldn't explain it, but she had me willing and ready to do better. Kels wasn't with the street shit and she made it known.

She was my peace. Lord knows I was going through it mentally. I wasn't a gangster and I never claimed to be. I got my bread and I stayed out the way. But, it was like, ever since Dre been on his rampage, my soul wouldn't settle and I didn't know what to do to make it right. Innocent people were losing their lives and we still didn't know where Ox was.

I let out a husky breath of air, as I stared at the screen of my phone. A part of me was ready to say fuck everything, but I couldn't give up on my crew. They were my family and we needed each other now more than ever.

A text came through from Rahdeek with three words: **The house. Now**

I knew exactly what that meant. It was time to ride out. He told us earlier that one of the soldiers may have gotten the drop on Ox, so we were supposed to be going to check it out tonight.

Peeling myself from the bed, I felt Kelsey's tiny fingers as they wrapped around my arm. I looked down at her face, then back to her hand. "What's up, beautiful?" I asked.

"Where are you going? I thought I had you for the night." We had just went two rounds. She fucked me like her life depended on it tonight. I felt her soul leap from her body and implant into my heart. I wished things were simple enough for me to stay in bed with her, but they weren't so I had to make my move.

"I'll be back," I told her, grabbing my shirt from the floor and pulling it over my head. "Just make sure you keep my side of the bed warm." I smiled, attempting to reassure her that I was good.

"Every time you leave in the middle of the night, you come back different, Camden. It scares me. I don't know what you're out there doing and I definitely don't want to ever get a call saying you're not coming back to me." Her lips formed a pout as her hazels sparkled back at me.

"Didn't I say I was good? I appreciate you worrying about me though, Kels. That's why I'm gon' give you my last name." I thought about it for a second and smiled. "As a matter of fact, didn't you say you was ready to get the fuck on from Michigan?"

She nodded. "Well, find us somewhere to go. I'm ready to make that move too."

Kelsey's face lit up and I swore I'd do anything in my power to keep that smile. "Stop playing with me, Camden. Move, how? Are we ready for that? I mean, I love you. I know I do, but a year isn't long enough to know if moving to a whole new state together is something we need to do."

"Well, unless you know something I don't, I'm in this shit until you don't want me no more? What, you ain't trying to fuck with me?"

She leaped from the bed and wrapped her arms around my neck. The wild bush on top of her head flopped in her face. Kelsey had me on some sucker shit. I didn't give a damn about another broad. I knew she was my soulmate.

"I love you, Camden. Please be safe. I'm so ready for the happily ever after. Between you and my brother, I can't keep up with the stress." Speaking of my brother, I want you to meet him. He's my everything and maybe you can talk him out of the streets too."

I frowned. "I thought I was your everything. Let me find out."

"You are, silly. You know what I meant. I want you to meet him. We're getting serious."

"I got you, ma. Set it up and I'm there."

Whatever she wanted, I didn't have a problem giving it to her. She didn't ask for much. So, I wanted to give her everything.

***

In the wee hours of the morning, Kelsey was the last thing on my mind. I was with the crew and we were parked in Rahdeek's Denali on the eastside of Detroit, checking out the scene. We watched as Ox's truck pulled in the driveway of the house that CJ cat was supposed to be at and two niggas jumped out. Dre was tripping.

"These niggas got the nerve to be riding around in her shit like fuck me. They don't give a fuck about me finding them, huh?" He pulled on the door handle, almost exposing us. "What the fuck we waiting for?"

Rahdeek grabbed his arm, stopping him. There was still a little tension in the air between the crew, but we all tried to put it to the side and come together for Ox.

"Listen, Youngin'," Rahdeek started. "We all anxious to get Ox back, but we got to do this the right way. We can just run up in there and put everybody in danger. We need a game plan."

"Fuck a plan. Kick the door in, snatch up Ox, drop everybody, and get the fuck on."

Rahdeek shook his head. "If it was that fucking simple, I would have did this shit on my own. Stop being so fucking bull headed and listen."

Dre's face screwed all the way up. "Yo', who the fuck you talkin' to nigga. I respected you because we do business together, but I'll fuck you up, nigga."

"Man, y'all chill out." I interrupted their pissing match. "We just got the closest we been in days to finding Ox I don't y'all not about to let y'all egos fuck it up."

"Well he need to shut up talking to me like I'm not a fuckin' problem." Dre grumbled.

Rah smirked. "You got that, youngin'. We all problems, but you ain't the enemy so I guess it really ain't an issue." He turned to Abe and the two cats we had rolling with us. "Look, y'all go knock on the door and when they open it, we rush them. Snatch Ox, do what y'all do, and let's get the fuck on."

"Yo', and be careful. It's babies in there. I'm all for getting Ox back. But I ain't trying yo kill no kids." KJ, the soldier that dropped the information in our lap spoke.

"Man, fuck them kids," Dre's ignorant ass frowned.

"Nah, it's not fuck the babies. I'm down with the crew, but I ain't with killing no innocent kids. My soul ain't tough enough for that shit." I admitted, not giving a fuck what they thought.

"Well, y'all just make sure y'all keep the little motherfuckas out my way. It's whatever," Dre cocked his gun and I pulled my hood over my head. I knew that tonight would weigh heavy on my soul like all the other nights. But, I mentally prepared myself for it.

***

Nothing ever went as planned; especially when everyone was running off emotions. When we burst through the door, we were met with hot lead whizzing past our heads. It was complete chaos. Bodies were dropping, people were screaming, and I couldn't do shit but play my position.

Pow! Pow! Pow!

The boom was deafening. I felt like we were in the old westerns. I tried my damnedest to stay low and get the kids out the line of the fire. Bur damn, I saw it before I could process it. The little boy's eyes bugged before his mouth opened, and his body dropped to the ground.

I choked. That wasn't supposed to happen. My entire body froze. We were in the middle of a war and my feet felt like cement.

"Yo', watch out." Abe pulled me to the ground and sent two shots behind us. "The fuck you doing? You almost got your dome busted."

I shook my head to shake the fog. "Y'all niggas just killed a baby, bro. That little nigga ain't had shit to do with this."

"Fuck that baby, nigga. We got to get the fuck on."

A few more shots rang out before all the shooting stopped. When it was all said and done, two niggas, a woman, and a baby were dead. This shit was crazy.

"Y'all ma'fuckas killed everybody!" Dre yelled. "Ox ain't here. How the fuck we supposed to find her now?" He ran his hands through his rugged hair, pacing. "Fuck, man. This some bullshit!"

"Youngin'," Rahdeek tapped Dre's shoulder. "We got to get out of here before them blues pull up. We hot as hell." He wanted, turning to face Abe and I. "Let's go!" He demanded, fast walking to the door. We all followed, but I had to take one last look at the chaos we created. I knew the scene would haunt me forever.

Chapter Nine

Ox

"Man, I'm telling you. Them ma'fuckas ran up in my bitch shit and laid everybody down. This broad got to go. Fuck the money. Fuck everything!" CJ paced the floor and my heart stung with fear and hope.

I knew my baby wouldn't give up on me. He was close. I just hoped that he found me before they finally killed me. This last week had been hell. They beat me so much that I was numb to the pain. They'd done everything imaginable to disrespect me besides rape me and I was ready to give up... until I heard my baby's name. Dre was going to save me.

"How you know it was them?" Sunny asked.

"Because I was there, my nigga. That bitch ass nigga Dre and his peoples." He looked over at me with a scowl. "I respect you Bossman, but this bitch time is up. Man-Man already gave me the go."

Sunny shrugged. CJ walked over to me, lurking menacingly. "You bout to die bitch! They gon' find you down river somewhere."

“Do it then.” I whispered. I was tired of fighting and too weak to protest. He had kicked, punched, slapped, and pissed on me for a week straight. If he was going to kill me, I wished that he get it over with.

Slap!

“Still so much fucking mouth.” The sting to cheek only lasted a second. He began to rein blows on me like a nigga in the street. I prayed it would stop. But knowing how this fucked up life of mine was set up, God was gone say fuck me fasho.

Bam!

A blow to my temple sent my head flying back and my vision became blurry. I felt myself slipping in and out of consciousness. This was it. My entire life was full of pain. Maybe if they killed me, I would finally experience peace.

“Yo! Chill out bro.” I heard Sunny’s voice, but I couldn’t see him. My whole body was throbbing. I was sure he’d broken something. “Chill the fuck out, bro. You not about to do this shit in my crib. Know what? Go upstairs. We bout to ride out. You can handle that shit later.” Sunny instructed. He added a little more base in his voice.

I wondered why he kept stopping him. Every time the beatings would get too brutal, he would step in and stop it. He wasn't getting no fucking points from me for being a half ass captain save 'em. I was ready to die. I was over this bullshit.

Several minutes later, I heard the front door slam shut. Then footsteps began to make their way toward me. I thought for sure that CJ was back to finish me off finally. But it wasn't him. It was Sunny.

He pulled his knife out, flipping it open. Confusion and fear filled me, until he cut the rope around my wrists, then my ankles.

"Look, I'm gon' leave the back door open. If you here when we get back, I'm not responsible for what happens." His voice was even. Sunny never expressed emotion when he spoke. He stood and I looked up at him. He was rocking a fitted turned to the back over a jersey to match. I had never even looked into his face the entire time. But, I couldn't help staring. I had to study him for sincerity.

"Why? I saw your face." I managed to mumble.

He smirked. "And I know how to handle mine." He tapped his waist. "Just get the fuck on. This shit ain't for me or you." With that, he walked off and out the back door.

As soon as I heard the engine purr, I tried to peel myself from the ground, but my legs wouldn't move. I panicked. I had to leave. God must have heard me ask for a way out, so I prayed he gave me strength to move.

Mustering up as much power I could find, I lifted my body from the ground. One of my legs had to be broken, but I ignored the pain as tears slid down my cheeks. I was determined to live. I had to get out and make it back to Dre.

I had to... I had to...

"Oh my God! Are you okay, baby?" I heard a woman. I think it was a woman. Everything went black before I could even process it, though. The fight was over.

Chapter Ten

Dre

The foreign number that kept buzzing my line was about to annoy the fuck out of me. Whoever it was, they wouldn't let up and I wasn't trying to talk to nobody. I felt my world crumbling, literally. The night before was our only hope at getting Ox back and we fucked it up.

Pulling my truck into Flamingo liquor store's parking lot, I hopped out taking a hard pull from the blunt I'd been smoking. I needed to grab a pint of Remy and another blunt. I couldn't get high enough to ease my frustration. I was surprised I didn't get alcohol poisoning or overdose on all the liquor and weed I had took to the head.

The alcohol helped ease my mind and the weed made me not give a fuck. I was scared to be sober. The thoughts going through my head weren't normal.

"What up Dre?" My homeboy, Juan, slapped fives with me as soon as I walked into the store. He shook his head. "My bad about Ox. I know-"

Before he could finish his statement, I whipped the burner out and had it aimed at his head. "You know what? The fuck you speaking on her for if you ain't trying to tell me where she at? You know somethin' nigga?" I gritted, ignoring the gasps and stares of the ma'fuckas inside the store.

"Na... nah, bro." He stuttered. "You know I ain't even cut like that. You been my mans too long. This ain't even us. You tripping."

I had my finger on the trigger, ready to pop a shot in his head. My chest tightened. I knew I was on some bullshit. This was the exact reason I needed to get my liquor and find me somewhere safe to tuck myself until I was in my right mind.

I took Juan in with a frown. "You right. I'm trippin'. Now get the fuck out my face and keep Ox's name out yo' mouth."

I walked off, leaving him standing there looking at me like I was crazy. I was out of my mind. It was fuck the world.

My cell buzzed again as I made it to the counter. I sent the call to voicemail before taking in my surroundings. Everyone was looking stuck... like they didn't know whether to run, call the police, or stay in place. "The fuck y'all looking at?" I growled. "Yo' Mo. Give me a pint of Remy and a pack of White Owls."

Mo's eyes squinted on me. He was a cool ass Arabic dude. He'd been around for years and knew everybody in the hood. "You can't just do that, my friend." She shook his head. "You put me in a bad spot. You bad for business, my friend."

I didn't respond to him, instead, I peeled two twenties out of my pocket and snatched up my ringing cell phone.

"What?" I answered aggressively. Obviously, the caller didn't care that I wasn't in the mood for talking.

"Ummm... is this... is this DeAndre?" The caller stuttered. She was older. I could hear it in her voice. But, I didn't understand why she was hitting my line. I started to hang up, but something told me to hear her out.

"Who this?"

"I'm at the hospital with Oxty... Oxtanavia. She wanted me to call you."

My heart fell to my toes. I squinted. I had to be hearing wrong. I prayed this broad wasn't playing with me; for my own sanity. "Oxtavia?" I asked for clarification.

"Yes, baby. We're at Providence on 9 Mile. Found her outside. She was beaten up prett-"

I hung up. There was nothing more to say. I needed to get to my rib.

***

I didn't remember making it to the hospital or finding Ox's room. All I could focus on was her all broken up and bruised. Her eyes were swollen shut and the lumps on her forehead was evidence to how bad she had suffered. I swallowed, attempting to control the anger building up inside of me. My name wasn't DeAndre if I didn't find every single person involved and make them pay.

Ox slept peacefully as I sat by her bedside, holding her hand. I wanted to wake her up, just to hear her voice. But, I knew she had been through a lot. So I didn't want to disturb her rest. This shit was like a dream to me. I couldn't get lose enough to her. It was almost as if, she would disappear if I blinked.

I felt the pinned up aggression leaving my body as I watched her chest fill with air, then collapse. All the strength I had was depleting. For so long, I had to put up this image that I was tough and had everything together. Truth was, I was tired of being tough. I broke, allowing tears to fall from the depths of my soul. I cried for myself and Ox. We never got a chance to experience peace. We never got a chance to simply live. It was like, how much could one human being take?

"She loves you," The voice came from nowhere. I immediately wiped my face and put on my resting bitch expression. "I can feel your love for her too, DeAndre."

I frowned, recognizing her voice from the phone. She was an older lady with salt and pepper hair and deep brown skin. Her face was angelic, giving off genuine vibes. I wasn't trying to be rude, but I wasn't in the mood to entertain a stranger and I definitely wasn't in the mood to share Ox. I needed her all to myself.

"Whatever you two are into," The old lady kept going when I didn't speak. She walked further into the room. "God put it on my spirit to comfort y'all and wrap my arms around y'all. He to-"

"No disrespect, but fuck God. Look at her. If he cared so much, why the fuck we laying here?"

The old lady smiled. "Your mouth is horrible. We got to work on that. But, I want you to let that aggression go. So, I'll ignore it. It's okay to fuss and question his will, son. Even I don't understand certain things. But I'll tell you this then I'll leave you alone. For the night. If God didn't care about you, you wouldn't be breathing baby. We can put ourselves in these dangerous predicaments then get mad when he don't come when we want him to rescue us from our own decisions. I want you to think about that and tell Oxtavia I'll be back to visit her."

I watched her back out of the room. I thought about what she said, quickly dismissing it. There was nobody alive that could tell me that God cared.

***

The sound of monitors beeping woke me up and out of my sleep. It took a second to get my bearings together. However, once I did, I realized where I was and a smile crept on my face as I locked eyes with Ox. She was finally up and staring at me. She smiled even though it looked like it pained her to do it.

“I heard you crying, nigga. Big Bad Dre was crying like a little baby,” she teased. Her voice was scratchy and low.

I smiled too. “Don’t tell nobody. Shit, my eyes was sweating.” We both chuckled before my face straightened. “Seriously, Ox. You good? I was losing my shit without you, girl. You ain’t just some broad. You my best friend and my whole fucking lifeline. I thought you left me.”

“I don’t want to talk about that,” her voice was a whisper. It cracked as she spoke. It was eating me alive not to be able to take away her pain.

“We don’t have to talk about it now. Who was that old lady?” I asked changing the subject.

Ox shrugged. “My angel. She found me and brung me here.”

“Why everybody on that God shit today? We probably the most loyal and chilliest niggas on the planet but foul shit keep happening to us? Nah, I don’t want to hear it.”

“God has to test his shepherds. If he didn’t think you was strong enough, he wouldn’t put you through it, son.” It was the old lady. She was standing against the doorframe with a bag of food. “You don’t have to always see him to prove that he's there. That's why the teacher is always quiet through the test."

I started to say something slick, but Ox squoze my hand for me to shut up. "That's right, Mrs. Thompson. Dre said you was coming back later. I'm fine. You can go back and get some rest."

Mrs. Thompson waved Ox off. "My soul couldn't rest. I was too worried about you and this young man. It was meant for us to cross paths."

She sat on the other side of Ox. We kicked it for a little before I finally decided to call the crew. I never had a real, genuine mother or father figure. She definitely gave those vibes. Ox and I needed positivity. We were liable to crack.

Chapter Eleven

Abe

"My motherfuckin' nigga," I smiled as my cousin and I shook hands and locked in an embrace. He had just gotten home from a ten-year bid and ain't shit changed but his shoes. Los had always been a getting money nigga. So, when he pulled up on me in the big body Benz, I knew what was up.

"What's up, lil' cuz. The streets said you was the man to see. Y'all getting' it in."

I waved him off. I wasn't doing bad, but if Cherish didn't open back up the traps, my money was going to dry up. I had bossed all the way up and there was no way that I would go back to being a regular ass nigga.

"Nah," I shook my head, leaning against his ride. "Some crazy shit went down and the connect on some bullshit."

"Damn. What tip he on? You straight?"

I looked off. "*She* in her feelings on some female shit. Fuck that, I see you shinin' cuz. I'm tryin' to get like you." I smirked as a big booty chocolate broad walked by, swaying her hips.

"Damn, that ma'fucka thick as fuck. I missed that shit, cuz. I been knockin' down a different broad every day of the week since I got home and puttin' them to work."

I rubbed my hands together, before focusing on Los. “Fuck a broad. Until we get back right, I’m trying to make some money. What kind of play you got on the floor?”

Los smiled. “I just told you nigga. Pussy. Them bitches making me rich and I ain’t got to be ducking and dodgin’ lookin’ over my shoulders either.”

“Straight up?” A brow furrowed.

“Hell yeah. I don’t fuck with peons. Got the lawyers, politicians, and athletes on call. Them freaky ass niggas pay top dollar for pussy. I’m talkin’ one broad can bring home ten bands in a night fuckin’ with these cats.” He tugged on the hairs of his beard. “You know what, find you a few broads and I’ll put you on.”

I nodded. I knew a few chicks that would be down for making some paper. “Yeah, I’m wit’ it. Let me put a few plays together and I’ll holla at you.”

My phone buzzed with a call from Dre as Los and I slapped fives and he pulled off. “What’s up, bro?” I answered.

“Do I sound like a nigga? Why everybody up here to see me but my nigga, Abe?”

I couldn’t even help the smile that crept on my face. It felt good hearing her voice. “Ox? Man, stop fucking with me.”

“What other broad gon’ be on his line? I’m at Providence. Come me see, nigga.”

“Providence? Are you okay?”

Ox sighed. “I’m breathing, so of course I’m okay. Just hurry up. We waiting on you.”

After I hung up with Ox, Yonni hit my line all excited. “They found my sister!” She squealed. “Where are you, Abraham?”

I chuckled. “On my way to the hospital now. Why you always clocking me, girl? I ain’t yo’ nigga.”

“Boy, bye. Despite what you try to unconvinced yourself, you’re all mine Lil’ Nuts. Stop playing with me,”

Yonni was the only broad that I kind of liked claiming me. I was digging the fuck out of her. She was a good chick, but I knew I wasn’t the nigga she needed. I was a dog and if the bag didn’t get right soon, I was going to be on everything Los was on. I never had a problem getting women, so I knew a few I could put to work.

***

It fucked me up to see Ox laying in that bed. I knew Dre was trippin’ too. He stood off in the corner, quiet as fuck as everyone kicked it. I started to walk over to him to chop it up, but Yonni grabbed my hand, causing me to focus on her.

We caught eyes and she smiled. “I just want you to hold me, Abraham. I’m trying not to be emotional but, I am. Look what they did to her.”

I focused on Ox again. She was kickin’ it with Cam and Cherish. Ox was the type of person that pretended to be strong as a defense mechanism. But, I knew her experience had to be traumatic. They fucked her up and whatever Dre was on, I was on too. The ma’fuckas had to take whatever was coming to them for that hoe ass shit they did to Ox.

"She a soldier. Ox straight." I said, wrapping my arms around her neck from behind, pulling her close. " You gon' get fucked up trying to be all over me." I let out a small laugh as Yonni sucked her teeth.

"I'm grown, Abraham."

"I can't tell. Yo' momma better stop playin' me. Keep her hands to herself." I frowned. I still couldn't believe I allowed her to snack me and didn't do shit about it. I respected Cherish, even though she was a bitch, but I was also a man. I knew it was a power thing. Her and her daughter had issues with trying to control shit.

She giggled. "She just wants the best for me. It's not easy being with us. Despite what you think, we had it hard before we finally got it right."

"Hard how?" I cocked my head to the side. "Yo' momma the plug. What, you hard a hard time figuring out what Louie bag you want?"

"You sound crazy. She wasn't born with the game in her hands, Abraham. She had to fight and prove her position and it was ten times harder because she was a woman. My mother has been beaten, degraded, and thrown to the side. Instead of folding, she stood tall. That's why she's so protective."

I studied Cherish. If she had been through some shit, she didn't look like it. She was flawless as fuck... but hardened. I figured being in charge made her that way. I never considered the fact that she had been through some shit.

"I can dig it. I'm just glad we got Ox back. Now we can get back to the bag and handle whoever got down on us."

Cherish hadn't paid me no attention until I said that. She looked up. "We're not opening back up."

My face tooted up. "What? We got a million dollar operation going and you just gon' shut it down?"

"I don't give a damn about that money. I trusted you to protect my daughter and y'all couldn't do that. Y'all still haven't handled the niggas who did it." Cherish screamed. She never lost her cool. It would have been more potent if she hadn't dropped a bomb.

"Daughter?" Ox asked what we all were thinking. "What do you mean, Cherish?"

Cherish stared at Ox. There was a glaze in her eyes but she was too stubborn to let it fall. "I finally found you and they allowed you to be hurt. I'm not putting you at risk again."

"Wait," Ox tried to sit up. Her face scrunched in pain. "What do you mean found me and what you're going to let them do to me. If you're trying to say what I think you're sayin', I think I been gettin' around pretty good. We made a mistake, but we ready to get back to the bag."

"You're not ready to do nothing, Oxtavia!" Cherish shouted. "Getting to know you over the past few months has been everything and I don't expect to come in and drop this on you and have a Brady Bunch happily ever after. We have a lot to work on. But, what I won't do is put you at risk again, as your mother first and a friend second."

Ox shook her head. "No! You don't get to do this to me. Do you know what the fuck I been through?" Tears seeped from the creased of her lids. "I literally went through hell, my nigga! Hell. And you think you can come in here and dictate some shit now!" Ox was screaming and Dre finally stood standing by her side, concerned.

"Yo', y'all need to leave. All y'all got to go. She been through too much for this bullshit. Now ain't even the time, real talk."

Cherish stared at Dre. I knew she wanted to say something slick, with her mean ass. Instead, she nodded. "Understood. We have to talk Oxtavia. I know I have explaining to do and you have questions. I'll be in contact with you." She turned to Rahdeek and they both walked out.

I pushed off the wall, slapping fives with Cam and then Dre. "Alright y'all. I'm out. I got to find a way to get this money. I can't stop 'cause the bag slowed up."

Yonni followed me out of the room. "Wait for me. I'm going with you, Abraham. Let me just tell my sister goodbye."

I shook my head. "Nah, ma. I got moves to shoot. I'm gon' hit you in a minute." I didn't have time to play with Yonni today. I had to get back to the paper.

Chapter Twelve

Cam

In the weeks following Ox's kidnapping, the streets had been a warzone; complete chaos. The city's murder rate had been climbing. Nobody was safe. Dre hadn't rested since he found Ox. Quite frankly. I was tired of all the bullshit. We wasn't God out this bitch. We didn't get to decide when a ma'fucka took his last breath.

Ever since we ran up in CJ's crib and that baby had gotten laid down, I hadn't been right. It was like my soul couldn't forgive me, it wouldn't let me rest. Every time I closed my eyes, I saw that baby.

Cherish still hadn't opened the spots back up yet and I was cool with that. My money was decent. Plus, Kelsey had been looking into cribs for us to stay down south. She wanted to move to Atlanta, but I was thinking Florida or somewhere that way. As long as I got out the city, I was good.

The thought of leaving Detroit never crossed my mind until recently. I said I was going to be a Dexter nigga until I took my last breath. But, shittt, fuck that.

"Why are you so quiet Camden?" Kelsey stood in front of me, placing her hands on her thick hips.

I smiled, grabbing her waist bringing her to me. "Because, ain't much to say. I got the baddest chick in the game rocking my chain."

Kelsey blushed as I pecked her cheek. We were down at Chene Park at the R&B Takeover. Dru Hill, Jagged Edge, and Monica were set to perform and she just had to come. I wasn't tripping because I fucked with Jagged Edge and Dru Hill. Plus, I loved spending time with her. I knew I would be wifin' her the minute she called herself checking me at the Coney Island. Lil' momma had me open at first sight.

"You are such a finesser." She shook her head, tucking the stray strands of hair that had fallen on her face behind her ear.

"Finessin?" My head cocked. "what I need to do that for? I done had you already, not only had you, I wrote my name on them wall's in that pussy. I've been keeping it a band with you my baby."

"Have you?" She playfully raised a brow.

"You're making all these plans to take me out the state. But you still haven't met my brother and I barely see you anymore." Her lips formed a pout and I leaned in, kissing them. Kelsey had the softest lips.

"My bad. Shit been crazy in these streets. I got you though. I promise."

"Crazy how, Camden? I pray you're not out there doing things that can land you in prison or in a grave. Don't let me build my hopes up around you painting this happy ever after picture just to shatter my soul."

What I had been doing over the past few weeks was beyond foul. I'd done a bunch of shit I said I'd never do. I wasn't no killer or no gangster. That's why I stayed in my own lane sacking money off weed and getting the fuck out the way. I knew that when we got down with Cherish, it would put us in a different league. It introduced us to shit we never thought was possible. Upgraded us from workers to a boss of our own life. Nothing ever lasted forever I was dumb enough to believe our run would. I just didn't think it would end with an explosion.

I tugged on the hair of my beard. "Nah, I'm good. I got us, Lil momma." I lied, knowing nothing would be eight until we got the fuck on.

***

After the concert, we were headed back to Kelsey's crib. I had been feeling on her fat ass all night and I was past ready to break her back. My solider was at full salute just thinking about her.

"Your phone is ringing, Camden." Kelsey said, snapping me out of my thoughts. "It's yo' baby momma." She smirked.

I chuckled. "Chill out. You know what's up." I warned before pressing my phone to my ear.

"What's up Tiff?"

"Cammm," She cried into the phone hysterically. "Please come get my babies. I'm going to jaillll." I could barely comprehend what she was saying as I turned the radio down.

"What? Calm down. What happened?"

"He... he tried to rape my baby! I stabbed that ma'fucka, Cam. They gon' lock me up." Tiff completely broke down on me. I wanted to ask her more questions, but I knew I needed to get to Sha.

"Where you at? I'm on my way."

"Home. Please hurry. I'm bout to call the police and they gon' lock me uppp."

I hung up, banging my fist against the steering wheel. Sha and her brother were my hearts. I didn't give a damn what me and Tiff went through. Sometimes I hated her dirty ass. I bet she brought some new nigga around them babies, putting them in danger. I thought about how she moved me right in with the kids after only knowing her a week. Fuck, some broads didn't deserve to conceive babies.

***

When Kelsey and I pulled up to Tiff's crib, she was sitting on the porch, cradling the kids. Her face was puffy and her hair was a mess. Sha saw me first. She peeled herself away from her mother and ran to me, wrapping her arms around my legs so tight it felt like she thought I would disappear if she let go.

"Uncle Cam. He hurt me." She cried. "You promised me you was coming back and he hurt me." Her body was shaking violently as I carried her to the porch with her mom and brother. My heart turned to steal. My blood was boiling. I tried to remain calm; just until I figured out what was going on.

"Where he at?" That's the only words I had as Tiff looked up at me. I couldn't front. I wasn't in love with her, but I cared about her. So, seeing her so vulnerable did something to me.

She pointed to the door. "In there. I lost it. I saw him on top of my bab..." Tiff paused mid-sentence. Squinting as if it would help her see better. "I know you didn't bring this bitch to my house!" Her voice squeaked. "You brought this hoe to my crib?"

She hopped up and started running toward my car before I had the chance to process what was happening. I didn't have time for this bullshit. I shook my head, placing Sha on the porch and making my way to the car.

"Get out the car you homewreckin', bitch. I been wanting to beat that ass." Tiff screamed.

I grabbed Tiff's arm. "Chill out, girl. Ain't nobody about to fight you. We got serious shit going on."

"Nah nigga. You call yo'self bossin' up and leaving me, and you fucking with the ops. Stupid ass nigga."

I frowned. Leave it Tiff to call me over to help and turn it all around on me.

"Stop talking crazy. Look at yo' daughter Tiff. Look at the example you setting. You supposed to be comforting that baby. You got a nigga laid dead up in yo' crib, but you worried about who I'm fucking?"

I could hear sirens in the distance as they came closer. My tongue ran across my lips as I took Kelsey in. She calmly sat in the passenger seat of the ride as Tiff went ape shit. "No you made it a factor Camden. You brought this bitch around me! My child was raped, nigga. It's a man laying up in my floor. You think I want to see this hoe."

Kelsey pushed the door open. "Camden. Get her, or get me away from here. I don't appreciate being put in this predicament."

"Fuck yo' predicament, you scandalous bitch. This right here gone always be a part of me. I don't know what yo' dizzy Dora ass did to make him so blind. But when he finally wake up and realize you're the ops. I hope he put a bullet in yo' fat head."

I pushed Tiff back toward the house. "Yo' kids out here. Go be a mother Tiff." I turned to Kelsey.

"Give me a second. Just get in the car ma."

I couldn't believe the chaos threatening to unfold. I didn't know how much more I could take.

***

After everything was said and done, Tiff ended up having to be taken to the station and the kids went with me. Kelsey was tight as fuck too. She wasn't feeling the kids at all. So, I dropped her off and went back to the crib after ordering pizza. These babies were innocent and I was the only father figure they knew. Plus, after what I been through these past few weeks, I knew it was my obligation to protect them.

"Uncle Cam." Sha's voice snapped me out of my thoughts. I turned to face her. At nine, she was growing up way before her time. Her mother was so busy chasing dick and dollars that she forgot to be a mom. Even with me, when I first got with Tiff, I had to make her love them babies. I barely knew her and was laying up in her bed.

"What's up, Sha?"

"Why you leave us? When you was there, nobody hurt us and momma was happy,"

Damn, I knew she was too young to understand the real. It wasn't me that messed everything up. It was her momma.

I shrugged. "Sometimes stuff happens, Sha. Your mother wasn't happy with me."

"Yes she was. Now she cry every night because you with your enemy and not her. She said you don't love us no more. But I know you do."

I shook my head. Tiff was fucked up for poisoning this little girls head. "Kelsey ain't the enemy, Sha. And you right. No matter what, I got yo' back. You gon' always be my baby girl, okay? Pinky promise."

Sha smiled. "I got your back too. If that girl try to kill you again, I'm gone kill her first."

My brows furrowed. "What girl?"

"Her. Momma said you got beef with her family and you still messing with her because she put voodoo on you. She poisoning you and I'll kill her if she put voodoo on you again."

I held in a laugh. I remember when I first met Tiff's kids. I wasn't trying to connect with them. I wasn't trying to connect with Tiff either. But these babies became apart of my heart.

"Stop listening to everything your mother say, Sha."

"Well, is she coming home or am I going to have to stay with you?"

I thought about it. What if they locked Tiff up? I wasn't ready to be no daddy to the next nigga's kids. But having them around may have been the escape I needed to get my mind away from the bullshit. I needed to get my shit together.

Chapter Thirteen

Dre

I sped through the city with Ox to the right of me. The Diplomats blasted through my speakers as we passed a blunt filled with Detroit's finest herbs. We didn't really have a destination in mind. We were just chilling and smoking.

"So, what are we going to do about getting product?" Ox interrupted our silence as I hooked a left down Dexter from West Grand Blvd.

"We ain't gone do shit. You need to relax, ma. Learn how to sit back and be taken care of for once." I shot.

Ox's ambition was something I loved about her. She wasn't a prissy chick either. She was perfect. Fine as fuck without having to flaunt it and she was smart. She was my best friend and probably the only person in the world that understood the way my fucked up brain worked.

Ox sighed "Here you go with that. I'm not the sit at home type, Dre. I'm a ma-"

My brows furrowed, knowing exactly what she was about to say. I took her in, the slick ponytail pulled to the back, the jogging suit and Jordans. She had that tomboy swag like Aaliyah used to rock. I licked my lips. Lord knows I was digging her hard. But, her mind was still damaged. I knew Ox was dealing with a complex. She had to be tough so she wouldn't appear weak. I wished that she understood that as long as she was by my side, wasn't shit weak about her. I was her strength and she was mines too.

"You a what?" I asked, once she didn't continue. "A woman? Last time I checked, the only dick you was working with was mines." I corrected her, making her blush, reminding me of her innocence. I knew she wasn't ready to be intimate with me and I wasn't rushing her either.

I smiled. "Don't worry, you good until I know you can handle a nigga like me."

Ox rolled her eyes. "You're so cocky. I swear. First off, you know what I meant. I've held it down for so long that I don't know how not to. I'm not willing to give up my independence because we're together."

"Who's trying to take yo' independence? After that shit that happened, all I want to do is protect you from the outside world. I'll really lose my marbles if some shit happens to you again. You my rib Ox."

'That's weird." She giggled. "This whole thing is weird. But I love it."

"You love it or me?" A brow raised

"Both. Now seriously, what are we going to do? I can't deal with Cherish...my mother...or whoever the hell she is." She sighed. "Do you know the hell I've been through while she was out being the queen of the streets? I was ruined. She don't get to come back into my life now that I don't need her."

I saw the tears welling up in Ox's eyes. I reached over, grabbing her hand, kneading at her knuckles. "Shit happens. Ain't nothing we can do to change it. I had a crackhead for a mother, bro. You know how much fuck shit she did to me? But I fucks with her because she my blood. She sober now too and I can accept it because I never gave up. I'm not fucking with Cherish right now either. But you don't know what that lady been through."

"What about what I been through?"

"I ain't trying to be on no unsympathetic shit. But let that shit go. We literally ain't got nobody in these streets, bro. We both been fending for ourselves for so long. Why not accept a ma'fucka that genuinely care?"

Ox eyes began to sparkle. I knew she was about to cry. "She don't care about me."

"You sound crazy Ox. That ma'fucka loves you. That's how I know some foul shit had to have went down for her to just say fuck it."

"Whatever." Ox muttered as her finger pointed out the window. "There go Abe. Who them clowns with him though?"

My eyes squinted to see who she talking about. Abe was chilling on a porch with three cats I didn't recognize. I didn't trust new faces.

I started to keep it pushing, but when Abe threw his hands in the air, I pulled to the side, stopping to kick it with him.

"Ox. Dre. What's up my babies?" He staggered to the car drunk as fuck.

I frowned. "Bro, you slipping. The streets too hot for you to be out here like this."

Abe frowned. "Man, I'm good in any hood, bro."

A brow raised as I took those new niggas in. "Are you sure about that? The fuck is them?"

Abe's neck craned back toward the porch. "Them?" He waved me off. "That's my cousin Nut. Just got out of prison, but he got a mean play on the floor. We just got to hop in."

I shook my head. "Nah, we smooth bro."

"You didn't even hear what the play is, bro. Fuck Cherish!" Abe turned to Ox. "No disrespect, sis. I know that's yo ol' bird. But, she ain't trying to let us eat. I need that rush I get from getting money."

"All money ain't good money, bro." I warned.

"I'm good Dre. Watch. Y'all gon' be wanting to get down too."

"Nah, I'm straight. Be safe my baby. Chill on the drinking though, no lacking." I slapped fives with him before pulling off.

"I don't trust them ma'fuckas. They seem shady, Dre. Abe is my brother. But, he's too flashy and flamboyant. That's why he's unbalanced."

I shrugged. "That's a grown ass man, Ox. He gon' do him. We just got to be here if shit ever get heavy."

Ox frowned. I felt her staring. "Are you serious right now, boy? That's family. I've never heard you say that. Like you don't care."

"I do care. But sometimes you got to reevaluate certain shit and know what matters the most. Losing you made me look at life different. Fuck these streets and fuck the bag too. I'm a real nigga. We'll figure it out."

"That simple?" Ox smiled.

"It got to be. That's why I said go holla at Cherish. Life too short to be holding on to grudges. My momma clean again. You 'bout to let me pop that cherry, and you found yo' momma. Fuck it.

"What?" Ox's nose crinkled.

I smirked. "You heard me."

Ox looked off. "I knew sex comes with a relationship. But I haven't really wrapped my mind around it. I'm scared, Dre."

"Scared of what? You know I'm just fucking with you. I ain't pressed."

"That's the thing. I want you to touch me that way."

Her voice got lower. "I want to feel you and it scares the shit out of me how much I'm letting you in."

I had to laugh at the way she blushed. "Look at yo' lil' freaky ass. I knew you was with the shits."

Ox chuckled "Shut up, DeAndre. Everything's always a joke to you."

"You ain't a joke at all. I don't play about you, lil' nigga."

"I know. That's why I love you and I'm almost scared to talk to you about what happened."

I let out a sigh, "Let me find out you Courage the Cowardly Dog. You shouldn't be scared of shit when it comes to me. I got you."

She bit down on her bottom lip. “I think Kelsey knows who snatched me. Seeing her at the hospital irritated my soul because I don’t trust her.”

“Why you say that?”

“Because one of them mentioned her name. I mean, I know she’s not the only Kelsey in the world and I know Cam loves her. So, I wanted to believe she’s good people. But, I just don’t know.”

I couldn’t respond. So I didn’t. Putting that charge on that girl would leave her body parts scattered around the city.

For Cam’s sake, I hoped Ox was wrong.

Chapter Fourteen

Cam

Kelsey's people had the block jumping. She had a big ass family and a part of me was feeling some type of way about meeting her people. We were getting serious, so it was inevitable. Something just didn't feel right. I just couldn't put my finger on it though.

"This ma'fucka packed." I mumbled, finding a space four houses down.

I wasn't trying to stay all night. So I was already thinking of my exit before I walked up. *This girl got me doing the most.* I shook my head, watching as two thick broads emerged from the background. They were pretty, just like Kelsey. I figured they had to be her cousins. One of them smiled at me as we caught eyes.

"Who you looking for handsome?"

I looked back to see who she was talking to before refocusing "Kelsey,"

"Humph, my cousin don't even look like yo' speed." She bit into her bottom lip. "I seen you before. Where you from?"

Man, Kelsey's people were wild. "Kels here yet?" I ignored her question. I wasn't with the messy shit. Baby girl was straight giving me the you-can-get-this-pussy face.

"She back there. For real, though. You look like you from my hood. I seen you before. You be over on Dexter near Joy Road?"

“Nah, not me, ma.” I lied, walking off to find Kelsey. That feeling in my gut wouldn’t go away and I hated that shit.

The barbecue was being held at Kelsy’s uncle’s house. It was a six bedroom mini mansion in the Sherwood Forest area. The ma’fucka was sick. I took in the landscaping as I pulled my phone to call her.

“The fuck this nigga doing at my people shit?”

“Yo’ nigga, you got me fucked up.”

I heard the side bar conversation and immediately turned to see who was talking. I didn’t plan to use the strap, but I was glad I had it on my hip.

“Cam! You made it!” Kelsey’s soft voice stole my attention before I could locate who was talking or who had a problem with me. Her arms wrapped around my neck. She smelled like flowers, honey, and good pussy.

I halfway hugged her back before focusing on the direction of those voices. Nobody was standing there anymore. Nah, I wasn’t feeling this shit.

I shook my head. “I just wanted to show my face. I got to shoot my move.”

Kelsey frowned, “You haven’t even met my big brother yet. He’s right there.” She waved her hand. “Manny. Come her.”

I turned to the direction she waved and almost had to do a double take. The fuck was Rick and his crew doing walking up on me? I saw the look on their faces. Kelsey set me up for a hit.

“Man,” Kelsey beamed oblivious to the danger lurking. “This my boyfriend Cam, Cam this is Manny. But our mom named him Rick.”

Kelsey’s brother was Rick? I didn’t know what to think. Before I could process it all, Rick whipped his burner out, Kelsey screamed, and I ducked behind an Escalade for cover. Bullets rang out like fireworks on the fourth of July.

“Fuck,” I cursed my luck, I had to get the fuck on. The beef wasn’t even me and Rick’s beef but I was guilty by association. I wouldn’t have had it no other way. However, what knocked the wind out of me was the fact that Kelsey set me up. All this time she had been calling her brother Man. I paused mid thought. Motherfuckin’ Rick was the main cat we was looking for.

He snatched up Ox and he probably sent Kelsey to fuck with me. All types of ill thoughts were running though my head. I fucked with Kelsey heavy. Tiff tried to warn me. Everybody knew I was fucking the ops but me. Damn.

***

I barely made it out that barbecue alive and quiet frankly, I didn’t know what the fuck to think. Lighting 3.5 grams rolled in a Fronto leaf. I took a hard pull, leaning back in my whip, waiting for Kelsey to pull up. She was going to have to tell me something because my first thought was to take her life. Shit had been crazy in the streets. There wasn’t no way she didn’t know nothing.

"Say you swear, bro." Abe's voice came through the car's speakers. I needed advice from my home team and I knew for a fact Dre wasn't the nigga to get it from. He wasn't in his right mind. Murder was the answer for everything with him.

"Man, if I'm lying, I'm flying. I wasn't even in that bitch two minutes before they got to shooting. Bro, she was like Cam, this my brother Rick, next thing I know he was pulling out the stick."

"That's fucked up. So what you gon' do about Kelsey? If she had anything to do with Ox. It's a wrap."

I took another long pull from the leaf, hating that my heart was involved. I still loved the fuck out of Kelsey, even though I knew she was possibly the enemy.

I watched as her car pulled up in the space two spots over. She wasn't even paying attention. She had this spaced out look on her face. I sat up. "Yo, I'll hit you later, bro. She just pulled up."

I hung up before he could respond, tapping the leaf out. Pulling my hoodie over my head, I hopped out with a scowl plastering my face.

"So you said fuck me, huh? This shit a game to you?" I snuck up on her, causing her to gasp, grabbing her chest.

"Omg. Camden! I'm so... so-"

"I don't want to hear that shit." I cut her off, stepping into her personal space. "You knew yo' people was beefing with my people, bitch."

"Bitch?" Kelsey's eyes opened with surprise. Normally, I would never disrespect a queen. But, tonight, fuck that queen shit.

"Camden, come on. This is me. I never knew that would happen. I care about you."

"Nah." I shook my head. "You don't give a fuck about me. I almost died fucking with you!" I grabbed her by her collar, whipping out my pistol.

Kelsey was terrified. She stumbled, but my grip was tight, not allowing her to fall. "Camden, baby." She gasped. "I swear, I wouldn't do anything to hurt you."

"Fuck that." I bit down on my bottom lip, feeling the gun handle shake. I wasn't no killer. That gangster shit wasn't for me. Staring into Kelsey's eyes, I knew murdering her wasn't for me either.

I pushed her back, tucking my pistol on my waist. "Stay the fuck away from me. Right after I put a bunch of bullet holes in that punk ass brother of yours, I might save a bullet for you." With that, I tightened the hoodie around my face, walking off. I couldn't even front, walking away from Kelsey was the hardest thing in my life to do, She had my entire soul.

Chapter Fifteen

Dre

"I expect to see you at the alter getting baptized next week," Pastor Bolden shook my hand as we filed out of bible study. This shit was new to me; praying, going to church, trusting new people. But, I was adjusting. I needed a change. I had been doing it so much my own way that it was only right that I at least tried to do this God's way.

Mrs. Thompson smiled. "I'm working on it Pastor. Baby steps. This one here is hard headed."

We all laughed as the sun hit our faces. "Nah, I ain't hard headed. This sh-" I paused, correcting myself. "I mean, this new to me. The whole praying and God thing. I guess I'm not too quick to jump on the bandwagon when all I've ever known is chaos."

Pastor Bolden smacked my shoulder. "Baby steps. Nobody is without sin. Remember that you don't have to be perfect for God to use you."

I nodded. I heard him but I was still getting used to this. Mrs. Thompson had us going to church, praying together, I was even plotting on a business to open up.

No lie. I felt better than I had felt in a long time. Everything was going right for a change. I was trying this preachy shit.

"What do you think about that, Dre?" Oxy asked as soon as we hopped into the Range.

“About what?” I questioned.

“Getting baptized. I want to do it. I need to do it.” I shrugged.

“I don’t know. I’m not with that holy shit. Then you really gon’ be trying to hold out on the pussy and shit.” Ox nudged me.

“Really nigga? Is that all you think about? I’m being serious, Dre.”

“Me too, shit. I ain’t ready to turn into a poindexter. I’m an original Dexter boy.”

“Whatever.” Ox giggled, pulling out her phone. She began to type on it and I caught her side profile. This ma’fucka had my heart in a vice grip. I’d literally lay down an die for Ox.

“Nah, for real. We can do it. I’m willing to walk to the end of the earth with you nigga.”

She smiled. “ The earth doesn’t end. Nice try. Can’t get rid of me that easily.”

I smiled too. “I wasn’t trying to. Look girl, this shit forever. Even in the after life, baby I will die for you like that Weekend song you like. I’ll fuck over any nigga that try to touch a hair on you.”

“Psycho, crazy ass.” She shook her head. “This thing we got is crazy as hell. I’m actually in love and have a boyfriend. Oxtavia Martin got a man.” She chuckled.

“Yep, a man that will do anything for you ‘cause I love the fuck out of you, girl.” My cell began to buzz before she could respond. I didn’t recognize the number, so I answered immediately, remembering what happened the last time I screened my calls. “Hello? Who this?” I answered.

“This is detective Oden Wallace. I’m looking for a DeAndre Martin. Son of Veronica Martin.” My heart began to flutter. I knew Ronnie would relapse. I didn’t even know why I cared as I prepared to hear the worst.” What she do this time?”

“I regret to have to inform you that Ms. Martin was fatally shot today in front of her home. You’re listed as next of kin, so we need you to come down and identify the body.” The phone dropped. The pain in my chest was almost unbearable. I had to pull the car to the side of the road. I became limp and could barely control the wheel. I couldn’t believe it.

“Dre, what happened? What’s wrong?”

“Somebody killed her.” I barely forced the whisper. I was sick.

***

A week later...

Numb and full of shock, I stood in front of my mother’s casket, watching as they lowered her into the dirt, silencing her forever. I didn’t understand this shit. I turned my life around.

I promised you, God. I was going to do things the right way, and you take my mother from me? My Cartier shade’s hid the single tear that leaked from my eye. I wasn’t even mad at the fuck nigga that shot her. Ronnie had been through hell and back fighting demons for years. She was finally going to have her peace. The fact that he took her away from me when I needed her the most had me fucked up. I was pissed at God.

I looked around. The whole hood had come out to show their love. Ronnie may have done her dirt, but everybody loved her. The crew sat to the left of me and Ox was to the right rubbing my back.

"It's going to be okay, Dre. Ronnie can finally breathe." She consoled me.

She was just getting herself together. I prayed for this shit and he took her? I shook my head, shrugging Ox's hand off my back. Then, I made my way back to the limo that was reserved for the immediate family. My crew and Ox was the only family I had left. I was really alone in this fucked up world.

I didn't even know that Ox had followed me until her soft voice called out to me. "DeAndre, wait." I let out a sigh. I really wasn't trying to be an asshole. Ox was my entire universe. I just needed to be alone to process this shit.

"What's up, beautiful?" I asked, stopping to face her. I had never seen her wear a dress before. Lil' momma was bad as fuck. She was rocking one of them form fitting black slingy dresses that stopped just above her knees, flat sandals, and her hair pressed with a part down the middle. I smiled at my universe. "Let me just get a minute to myself ma. I'm going through something right now."

Ox walked closer, closing the space between us. Her head pressed against my chest. She wasn't the affectionate type, unless she was on the receiving end and I immediately felt her presence.

"We're going to go through it together, Dre. You're not alone anymore, boy. You're my superman. Allow me to be superwoman." Her bright eyes looked up at me, staring into my soul. " I love you, DeAndre. More than you know. When you hurt. I hurt."

My heart began to beat wildly in my chest. This girl didn't even know what she did to me. Words couldn't express the depth of my love for her.

"That's why I'm gon' give you my last name and a couple of my legacies."

Her nose crinkled. "I can't be nobody's momma."

"You gon' be the dopest mom dukes on the planet, watch." I bit down on my bottom lip. "Thanks Ox. For just being he-.'

Before I could finish my sentence, shots rang out, sending bullets whizzing past our heads. I knocked Ox to the ground covering her with my body. I wasn't even strapped. We were trapped and if these fools decided to run up, I was assed out.

The funeral was in an uproar. People were screaming, babies and mothers were running, and as I crouched down protecting Ox, I got my confirmation. Fuck trying to change. I couldn't be a good nigga. Nah bro, I was going to have to be an animal; a fucking savage forever.

I punched the ground as the shooting came to a stop. Niggas really just shot up my ol' bird's funeral? They had life fucked up.

***

After the chaos at the funeral, we all met up at me and Ox's crib. I hadn't sat down or stopped thinking since we pulled up.

"Niggas really took it there, bro. They ain't even let my ma'dukes get in the dirt properly. Bro, I'm about to spazz all the way the fuck out!" I hit my hand in my fist, pacing.

"Dre, calm down, please. We don't even know who it was or what they were shooting at. All types of niggas were there." Ox tried reasoning.

I shook my head. "Nah ma. That wasn't nobody but punk ass Rick. He been breathing too long. Nigga should have been canceled."

"Yeah, I'm with you, bro. It had to be that nigga and he got to go. It's getting out of hand. You know he fucked up behind that one shit still." Abe turned to Cam. "Did you tell that bitch where we was holding the funeral? I don't know what kind of voodoo pussy she put on you bro. But that bitch shouldn't be still breathing but-."

"Man gone with that bullshit, I ain't fucking with Kelsey, but I know she wouldn't play us like that either."

I frowned. "Just like you knew she wouldn't set you up at that barbecue? Almost got that ass killed, nigga."

Cam pushed from his seat. "I'm not about to do this with y'all today. My condolences about Ronnie. But, I'm out."

He began to storm off. But Ox stopped him. "Were not falling out now. We need each other. We all we got. Cam don't go. Pressure got us ready to bust. We too solid for that."

Cam sighed. "Y'all gon' always be my niggas. It's never a broad before y'all. Don't question my loyalty. Kelsey, her brother, and anybody else can get it when it comes to my family."

"Enough said, my baby." I held out my hand for a five. We embraced in a brotherly hug before he made it out the house.

"Yo', we good. I need to clear my head. We need to meet up tomorrow," I told Abe and the couple of workers who had followed us to the house. "We got to make a move asap."

Chapter Sixteen

Cam

Why she have to do this to us? I grabbed Kelsey's hips firmly, slamming into her with all my might. Her pussy felt so good and the better it felt, the madder I got. Why couldn't I just get her out my system? My thrusts were lethal. I knew I was touching her esophagus.

"Wait, Cam. It hurts so good, baby." Kelsey gasped. Her back had a mean arch.

I couldn't explain how I found my way over her house and between her legs. The shit just happened and now I felt like I was at home inside her pussy. Kelsey was my peace and she had to go and fuck it up.

I felt the nut building up at the tip of my shaft, threatening to erupt. I didn't want to cum because I didn't want her to know that she had the only pussy I wanted in this world. Going deeper, I felt the goosebumps as they spread up my arms.

"Dammnit, Cam. I love you, baby."

Those were the magic words. Just hearing her say that caused my dick to go limp. She didn't love me. She almost got a nigga killed and I was slipping for being up in her crib, allowing my emotions to mask my better judgment.

I pulled out, taking a step back. I looked down at my joint, glistening with her using, then back at Kelsey.

She was confused. Her brows knitted together as she panted.

"Why did you stop, Camden?"

I shook my head. "Because I can't do this shit." I walked over to her master bathroom, grabbing a rag out the linen closet and turning on the water.

Kelsey followed me. "Hey," her soft voice called out. "You can't do what? You know damn well I had nothing to do with that? Why are you punishing us both?" I saw her blink back tears, hurt.

My intentions weren't to come hurt her. I just wanted to talk. But, when I pulled up and she threw herself in my arms, there wasn't no talking. I bit down on my bottom lip. "I don't know nothing and that's why I need to dead this shit. I can't fuck with you Kelsey. I'm gon' end up marking yo' brother and you gon' hate me."

She finally allowed the tears to leak from her cheek. "It doesn't have to be that way Camden. Let me just talk to him."

I shook my head. "It's too deep. Bodies done dropped behind this shit."

Kelsey fully made her way into the bathroom. She pressed her body into mine, wrapping her arm around my waist, and laying her head on my chest. "Where does that leave us?"

I shrugged as my heart raced. If I followed it, I would have been deep inside Kelsey, lying to her, promising that everything would be good. However, I couldn't make that promise. Shit was all bad.

I peeled her arms from around my waist. “It leaves us in a fucked up space.” I tugged at the hairs of my beard. “I know you didn’t have nothing to do with that shit. But, you saw how deep it is. I almost lost my life. I can’t fuck with it.”

After saying that, I stepped around Kelsey, grabbing them on, skipping a shower. I didn’t want to hurt her because I loved her. But, I had to get the fuck on before I suffocated.

***

Two days later, I had to block Kelsey's number. She called me all day, leaving messages. I hated to put baby girl through that, but I couldn’t fuck with her without hurting myself in the process.

“Uncle Cam. Uncle Dre is here.” Sha called out, making her way into my doorway. She stood there with those two lopsided ponytails I called myself putting in her head.

I frowned. “How you know? You wasn’t supposed to touch the door.”

Sha's little head dropped. “Sorry uncle.” She looked down in shame.

I grabbed her chin, pulling her face up. “Nah, you not sorry. Don’t ever say that. You just have to be careful. I don’t want you to touch the door because I don’t want you to get hurt.

She nodded and I ruffled those lopsided ponytails, standing to see what Dre wanted. I hadn’t talked to him since his mother's funeral. I wanted to give him space to think. Everything was fucked up.

Dre was pacing the living floor when I walked in. He didn't even notice me. "What's good, nigga?" I snapped him from his trance.

"I wasn't even gon' involve you, but we got to end this bullshit. At my momma's funeral, bro?"

I sighed. "I know," I paused, thinking about my next words. "So what you need me to do?"

Dre stared at me. "Call her. Tell her you want to holla' at her brother. I got the rest." I didn't say anything. What could I say? I had to choose between my bro and my fucking heart. I didn't want to shatter Kelsey's soul by involving her in her brother's death. But, it was what it was.

***

Kelsey had no idea what she had just put her brother in and a part of me wished she remained clueless. But, I knew better. As we loaded up to ride out, I knew that I was sealing our fate. If I caught her in the next lifetime, maybe circumstances would be different.

When I made the call, she seemed so anxious to hear from me. I told her that I needed her to set up a meeting with Rick so we could squash our beef. Kelsey called back with the location less than an hour later. I lied to her, knowing I was going to be fucked up behind everything in the morning.

The meet up spot was the park on Dexter and Waverly. We rode around the block, scoping the scene twice before pulling up. It was just past eleven o'clock and the park was empty besides two figures.

Dre passed me the blunt we had been rotating. “If you want to stay in the car, that’s cool bro. You did enough.”

My face twisted. “You sound crazy. We in this shit ‘til the wheels fall off.”

“My nigga,” Dre smacked fives with me. Then, he focused on Abe, Rahdeek, KJ, and another soldier named Rob. “We got to end this shit tonight, man. Make sure that nigga and any other nigga he brings with him is laid down.”

They nodded and we hopped out. Rick was standing in the middle of the park with some nigga. We really couldn’t see them, just the silhouettes. When we got close enough, Rick burst out laughing. “Y'all niggas stupider than y'all look.” He growled. He already had the pistol in his hand. “The fuck you thought this was? Ain’t no kissin' and making up. This shit real.” He lifted his pistol, aiming it at Dre's head. We heard pistols cock from every direction.

Damn, I wanted to believe with everything in me that Kelsey didn’t have nothing to do with this either... but I had to be a fool if I thought that. We were trapped, wasn’t nowhere to run. We could try to pull our tools, but they had the drop on us.

“This for Q,” Rick spat. However, tire screeched, the car door opened, and a voice yelled. “Mannie, wait. Don’t do this!” It was Kelsey.

In the heat of the moment, the distraction was welcomed. It was the piece of time we needed. Cannons got to blasting. We ducked for cover. We were in an all out war. The bullets weren’t picky, whoever got in the line of fire, they got hit. We were literally shooting for our lives.

It was so dark that I couldn't see who the enemy was or who was on the team. Things were getting heavy. My gun clicked but nothing spit out. I was out of bullets. Ducking behind the jungle gym, I fumbled with the clip, trying to reload. We had to get the fuck on before them blue boys came or a bullet hit one of us. "Fuck," I howled, frustrated, not knowing what was going on with my bros.

A gun cocked, it was close enough to jar my attention. "Punk ass nigga." I stood there, feeling as time stood still. I was about to die. I blinked, waiting for the bullet to pop. One second, I ask standing there, the next I was being knocked to the ground, the deafening boom of a gun went off. I wasn't hit and my trigger finger was ready. As I hit the ground, I aimed and fired.

I saw as the silhouette fell, bull the blood curdling scream touched my soul. "It was Kelsey who knocked me down. She scrambled, over to the silhouette. "Noooo! Mannie! Mannie, please." She cradled the body that I had just relieved of life.

I watched as she cried from the depths of her soul over her brother, the war around us slowly fizzling out, and the smell of death invading the park. One last bullet rang out before I heard Dre's voice. "Yo', Cam. Where you at nigga, you good? Cam!" He sounded frantic.

I couldn't stop watching Kelsey. When Dre found me, he tapped my shoulder, but I couldn't move. "Yo' we got to get the fuck on bro. It's handled. Let's go!"

I slowly drug my body off the ground. Damn, Kelsey saved me, only for me to be the one that pulled the trigger that ended her brother's life. I knew our fate was sealed and I prayed for forgiveness and mercy. Being without Kels was going to be hell.

Chapter Seventeen

Abe

Neisha was this broad I had been kicking it with before Yonni came trying to strong arm a nigga into being an honest man. She was thick as shit and her pussy was A-1. She had this innocent vibe that niggas would eat up. Plus, she would do anything for a nigga. I still remembered when she got her ass beat by Shabon on the block, that made her want a nigga even more.

I ran my tongue over my teeth as I watched her ass jiggle in front of me. We were at Mitch's off Grand River. I hadn't talked to her in months, but as soon as I offered to link up, she was down.

Los had the play together, I just had to get my own stable of broads willing to get this money together. I wasn't the nigga that could sit around and not get money.

"Damn, girl. You better stop playing with me like that." I leaned in and whispered in her ear. I was surprised she was being so loose. Neisha was the shy type.

She giggled, looking back at me seductively. "No, you better stop playing with me." She stood straight up and I led her to the back of the club and in a booth to kick it with her.

"So, what's been up Neisha? I wee you still looking good."

She blushed. “Thank you, Abe. I’m shocked you called. I really liked you and you played me.” Her lip poked out, forming a pout.

“Didn’t nobody play you. If anything, I was looking out. I ain’t shit, so I didn’t want to hurt you.”

She stared into my eyes for a second before responding. “So what changed now?”

I rubbed my hands together. “I got a play and I wanted to include you in it. I know you like nice things.”

Her brows furrowed. “What kind of play?”

I smiled. “Does it matter? I know you want to help us get this money. Ain’t nothing sexier than a chick a nigga can get money with.” I was laying it on thick. Neisha wasn’t a broad I saw myself being with. She was weak. I hated a weak broad... that’s probably why I was digging Yonni's crazy ass so heavy.

“Of course it matters, Abe. Just tell me what you have in mind.”

“Okay, I know a few rich niggas that loves pretty chicks. They just want to kick it and have a good time.”

“You want me to be a prostitute?!” She squeaked.

I chuckled. “Nah, I want you to be that bitch. Boss your life up. They paying top dollar just to spoil you for the night. I respect you, girl. I wouldn’t play you.”

Neisha looked off. Her leg began to rock as she thought about it. “Where would it leave us if I’m going on dates with other men?”

I shrugged. "We'll figure that out later. Is you trying to get this money with me or not?"

"You promise we can't talk about us later?" She sounded so naïve.

"Hell yeah. But look, I got something on the floor tonight. If you ready to ride with me."

"Tonight?"

"Yeah, are toy riding or you bullshitting?"

She sighed. "I'll do it, Abe."

I smiled. That's exactly what I wanted to hear. I needed two more girls that were down for me and I would be back to getting money. Pimping broads wasn't exactly my style, but the way I figured it. We both were getting off. Fair exchange was never robbery.

***

"Man, that broad handled her business like a champ." Los smirked. The night before, Neisha went on her date and I was picking up the money in the morning. I had my cousin drop her off her cut because I wasn't trying to see her yet. She was in her feelings and the past thing I wanted to do was be stuck consoling her. She wanted a relationship and I wanted to get this money.

Tonight, we were at this lounge on Seven Mile talking business. It was Los' spot. He was a getting money nigga but he was a drunk, which was sloppy. The only reason I fucked with him was because we weren't in no dangerous game. I swear, if we were in the streets, his wild ass would get us popped.

I shook my head, taking a hard pull from the blunt we had been burning. “I knew she would. Neisha will do anything for me.” I bragged.

“I can dig it, Lil Cuz.” He shifted in hit seat, sitting up as some big burly Higgs came marching over to our table. He looked mad as fuck and I was mad that o didn’t have my burner on my hip.

“Which one of y'all niggas is Los?” He barked.

Los smirked. “Who trying to find out?”

“A nigga that will kill about his wife. Got my girl out here on some monkey shit and-"

“Aye nigga. Don’t check me about no bitch because I ain’t put no gun to no broad's head.” Los barked, cutting the man off. The man lunged at Los, but the crew knocked his shit back so quick. They were mangling ol' boy so serious that I started to feel bad.

I tapped Los. “Man, chill. The nigga was in his feelings about his wife. Let him live.”

Los waved me off. “Fuck his hoe ass. He need to know to keep him and his hoe in check.”

The whipped ol’ boy's ass. I had to shake my head because security literally had to lift the nigga from the ground and carry him out. This was that wild shit I was talking about. Cuz was a nutcase. Fuck around and get us killed on some bullshit.

We kicked it for a few minutes before we all decided to leave the club. Man, why that nigga was waiting in the cut for us? We were met by the cool night's air and bullets. One barely missed my face and hit the nigga standing behind me. Damn, I saw my life flash before my eyes. I almost felt like I couldn't win from losing.

***

After the bullshit at the club, I decided to kick it with Yonni. I told her everything and of course her crazy ass wasn't with the new way I was getting money or almost getting shot at the club.

Her face twisted up. "First of all, you're on some desperate nigga shit. You don't have to be out here disrespecting women for money. That's a disgrace. Be a man. Find another plug, Abraham."

I waved her off. "How? You said that like it's that simple."

"It is simple. Plus, you know my mother isn't shutting down forever. She's just in her feelings right now. If anything, you know I got you."

I smirked. "Why you fuck with me so heavy? I'm just a regular ass nigga."

She rolled her eyes. "I ask myself that all the time. But, deep down, I think you love me. You're just scared to say it."

I chuckled. "How can I not love your crazy ass."

"You love me?" Yonni's voice cracked. She sounded like she was surprised to hear me say that.

"I mean, yeah. That's the only reason I tolerate your bullshit. But, I know I ain't shit. So I ain't trying to jump into no toxic relationship and have to fuck yo' momma up because I hurt you."

“That’s a cop out. In other words, you don’t want to man up and be the nigga you’re supposed to be. Plus, you can only do what I allow you to do.”

I smirked, leaning over to kiss on her neck. “You gon' allow me to get this nut?” I was tired of talking. My soldier was at full salute and I was past ready to be inside her.

***

I didn’t know how to man up and take responsibility for a woman. That’s why all I could offer Yonni was good dick and a little time. I put her ass too sleep after two hours of intense fucking. Now, I was up staring at my baby. I swear, if I was a better man, I would wife Yonni. She was fine as hell and she kept me on my toes. She looked so peaceful laying next to me.

My cell buzzed, interrupting my train of thoughts. It was Neisha. I heard her sniffling as soon as I answered her call.

“I can’t do that anymore, Abraham.”

I looked off, thinking about what Yonni said. I was on some desperate shit. I loved the ladies, but pimping them wasn’t my style. “You don’t have to. I appreciate you looking out, Neish.”

“So now we can be together?”

I blew out a breath of air, deciding to take the conversation to the next room so I wouldn’t wake Yonni. “Nah, I didn’t say all that. We chillin'.”

“Chilling?” She shrieked. “Do you know what I did for you? I gave my body to a stranger for you Abraham. I gave a piece of me away to make you happy.”

"Man, that wasn't just for me. You got paid, didn't you?"

"Fuck the money!" She screamed so loud I had to pull the phone away from my ear. "You know what, fuck it. I hate you. You're going to get yours." She hung up before I could respond and I was cool with that. I wasn't in the mood to argue about a decision a grown woman made.

Yonni was standing against the doorframe with her arms folded when I looked up. She shook her head. "You're wrong on so many levels."

I frowned. "Why you in my business?"

"You are my business, Abraham. And, what you did to her was wrong. You don't play on a person's emotions and manipulate them like that. That's how people end up on *Snapped*."

I waved her off and Yonni sauntered over to me, straddling my lap. "You act as if you don't care, but you should be. Every action has a reaction, Lil Nuts." I heard Yonni talking, but I didn't hear her.

Chapter Eighteen

Ox

I hadn't talked to Cherish since she told me she was my mother. I didn't exactly know how to feel about it. On one hand, I fucked with her heavy. She gave off those mother vibes. But, on another... I was pissed off that she left me with him. My life was fucked up and she didn't get the pass to just come back and pretend everything was all good.

My lips tightened as I studied her. "I was young, weak, and scared. Doug used to beat me for breakfast, lunch, and dinner. He degraded me every chance he got. I was a broken little girl, Octavia." She was explaining as I tuned back in. I had zoned out for a second, reminiscing on the years that my father intentionally tried to break me every chance he got.

I shook my head. "But, what does that have to do with me? You knowingly left me with a monster to suffer the same fate you did."

Cherish looked off. A tear rolled down her cheek. "I prayed that he would be better to you, considering you were his child. And, I prayed for the strength to finally stand up to him." She let out a small laugh. "As strong as I've become. He's still my only weakness. I just need for you to understand where I was coming from and forgive me. I want us to move forward. I know it takes time and healing, but I want to work on it."

"I have a lot of healing and understanding to do, Cherish. I can't even front." I looked off, taking in the picture of *my mother*, Rahdeek, and Yonni smiling like the perfect family on Deek's mantle piece. I pointed at it. "You see that? I didn't get to experience shit like that. On one end, I'm bitter as hell. On another, I just want to hug you and break down and finally breathe." My emotions had my last sentence coming out a whisper.

"This is hard for me, Cherish. We can't just move on like nothing happened. It's going to take time. But, in the meantime, don't make everybody suffer because of my mistakes. You're stopping everybody's money."

She shook her head. "I don't give a damn about nobody's money at this point."

"So, were you doing it to help or did you only help to get close to me?"

Cherish wiped her eyes. "I stepped in because I was finally able to offer you the lifestyle and protection you needed. I needed to be here for you."

"But you wasn't when I needed you most."

"And, I can't change that. We can only move forward with action."

I looked off. "He beat me... he degraded me... he left me so scarred that I have a great man and I don't completely know how to fully let him in because my wall is constantly up."

"I'll fix it."

"How?"

Cherish ran her tongue across her teeth. She shrugged. "The only way I know how."

I didn't even try to decipher what she meant. My pain was so deeply rooted that I knew there weren't a way possible to fix me.

***

Two days later, I was on the phone with Mrs. Thompson. Dre and I had been staying away from her because we weren't in the right head space for where she was trying to take us. However, I needed her pure unbiased ear. The thing with Cherish really had been weighing heavy on me.

Mrs. Thompson said a deep prayer for my peace and was talking to me about forgiveness when my line buzzed. It was Cherish. I sighed. "She's clicking in now, Mrs. Thompson. Thank you for praying with me, even though I know I'm hard headed." I chuckled.

"I know. But, I love you anyway. Have an open heart, an open mind, and stop questioning yourself. Call me later, Oxtavia."

By the time I tried to click over, Cherish had hung up. So, I dialed her back. She didn't even allow me to say hello. "Meet me on Dexter," She hung up before I could respond. I knew she was talking about the spot on Taylor and I wondered what she wanted.

It took me an hour to pull myself together and make it over to the spot. Rahdeek's Denali was parked in the driveway and the front door was open. There wasn't no telling what I was about to walk in the house to. However, I definitely wasn't prepared to walk into the house and find my father bound and gagged on the living room floor. When he saw me, his eyes bugged and he began to try to mumble something. Of course it was unrecognizable.

I frowned. “What’s this?”

Cherish focused on my father, her face tightened. “I call this righting my wrong and finally getting closure for the both of us.”

I shook my head, taking a step back. Seeing my father looking so vulnerable did something to me. I hated the chains he had me shackled to. In a way, I felt obligated to save him from the terror I knew Cherish planned to cause. In another, I wanted to take the gun from Cherish's hand and blow his brains out.

“I got closure when I left his wing, Cherish. He can’t hurt me anymore.” I lied to the entire room, including myself.

“No you didn’t. You’re still holding on to the same pain I have, Oxtavia. Neither of us will be free until he's gone.”

My brows furrowed. “So, are you doing this for you... or for me?”

Cherish's heels clinked as she made it over to me. She stood behind me, grabbing my hand and placing the gun in it. She held my hand up with hers, aiming the pistol at my father's head.

“Both. This ends today, Oxtavia. Our first step to moving forward is killing the toxicity binding us and we're going to do it together.”

I felt my entire body heat up and my adrenaline beat at my chest as I held the gun with my mother. Pops began to scream and squirm and my hands shook. “I can’t do this.” Tears began to seep from my eyelids.

“Yes, you can.” Cherish whispered in my ear. “We are going to do this together. Just pull the trigger

Ox. I'm with you every step of the way. I'll never leave your side again."

I squeezed my eyes shut so tight that they stung. "Squeeze it Ox. Free us." She urged me.

"I can't," I cried.

"Think of all the times he put his hands on you and beat you down mentally. Free yourself. Free us. Shoot Ox!" She squeezed my finger. The gun went off. I didn't mean it. I gasped as I watched my father's head explode. His body flew back and went limp.

Cherish pulled the gun from my hand, dropping it onto the table next to us. She turned me around and hugged me close, rocking me, and rubbing my back. "We're free Oxtavia. I love you. Never stopped loving you. I want you to come back to Virginia to live with me. There's nothing left here."

"I can't leave my crew. We have to get back to work. You have to open back up the spots."

Cherish sniffled with a smile. "After the breakthrough we just had, you're still worried about the crew?"

"My family," I shrugged, trying my best not to look at my father. As dysfunctional as we were, he was the only family I'd known for years.

"I'll give the order to open back up. But, seriously think about coming to Virginia. I'll make sure that you and DeAndre have everything needed." She wiped her face before focusing Rahdeek. "Call the boys to come clean this mess up, please."

I didn't say a word. I just cried. Seeing the life leave my father's body did free me and it hurt because I loved him.

***

The minute I walked into the house, Dre knew something was up. He rushed to my side and held me. "What happened, Ox?"

My shoulders rocked as I cried. "She killed him. I mean, we killed him."

"Who?"

"My father. He's dead DeAndre. I don't know how I'm supposed to feel about it. I never wanted to see him dead. But I feel relieved at the same time. Am I fucked up?"

"Hell, nah. Fuck that nigga. He had too many passes anyway." Dre grabbed my chin to make me look up at him. "You're not weak, never been. But, now you can move on and let me in. Just know, I got you and always will."

"I know," I looked off. "She's going to order the spots to start back running. We're back." I changed the subject.

Dre frowned. "Fuck them spots. Are you good, Ox?" He stood over me, his presence so powerful. Our faces were nearly touching and when he closed the space between us and our lips touched, my whole body felt like it went into shock. I had never felt the way I was feeling about anyone. I had never loved another human being and had it reciprocated.

Terror filled my chest. I pushed him away. "This is too much right now, DeAndre."

He sighed. “It's not enough. But, I’m on your time. It’s always about you so don’t ever forget that.” He pecked my lips again and I just rested my head on his chest, needing the closeness.

Chapter Nineteen

Dre

It was a good ass day. We were back in full effect. There was no feeling like getting to the bag and feeling like a boss in the process.

After Cherish and Ox squashed their beef, Cherish hit us with some fire ass shit that had the fiends lined up around the block. Ma'fuckas in the streets were saying it reminded them of some shit from the 80's, giving us even more power.

Things were being ran completely different this time. We had to make sure our operation was air tight. We beefed up our presence in the hood, and added more soldiers.

We needed to flex our weight so niggas didn't try no stupid shit. The crew had bought ten houses on one block. I mean, we had a few fixer uppers, but the dope we had probably was the same shit the Egyptians used to build the pyramids.

"Hey! Nephew, me and Freak Train's stanking ass done with all them bushes, trees, and grass. We painted one side of the garage cau-"

I stopped Cherry, one of loyal fiends, to make a long story short. 'Cause auntie could talk for hours. "Hold on, Ox." I sat my plate of food next to me. "Cherry, you mean to tell me y'all done with all that work in two hours?" I asked skeptically. Cherry was as slick as they came. You closed your eyes too long and she was getting over.

"Nah, nephew. I'm saying that we gon' finish later. I want to wave my rights to give both of us a one-an-one and some water." She said that shit like she was a lawyer fighting a case and the shit made any type of sense. She wanted to wave her rights to what? I chuckled. Auntie was tripping.

Then, she had the nerve to keep talking a bunch of shit I wasn't paying attention to. I couldn't help but to notice two Dodge Charger Hellcats; one was white and the other was red. They were racing around the corner, leaving the block in a blanket of smoke.

"What up though, bro, bro?" Abe yelled, halfway out the car door before his cousin and the driver behind them could stop.

“What’s good with you, bro?” I slapped fives with him, eye brows raised.

“Nephew! Can I go get it?” Cherry touched my shoulder impatiently. “Hey, Abe.” She waved. I didn’t miss working the block and I didn’t plan to be on the forefront for long. We just had to make our presence felt and niggas knew not to test me.

“Yeah, Cherry, go head. Tell lil’ cuz I said yeah and make sure y’all finish up. I’ll have Rhonda fix a couple plates of barbecue and something to drink.” I directed her, focusing on the entourage falling out of every door of both cars.

“Abe, this ain’t River Rouge. Can’t pull up on the block like this. This a place of business, bro. Y'all got to raise up.” I frowned. It was never fuck Abe, but I wasn’t feeling his cousin. He just seemed like a sketchy ass nigga.

“Dre! You always tripping. Cuz fresh out. You could smell the chicken on the grill from a mile away. Nigga we cousin Pete, came to eat.”

Abe’s double foamed cup was a dead give away of why he had been thinking so irrational lately. His cousin probably was into some paper but it was a bad influence on Abe.

“What up though? They call me Los. Abe said I should bridge with you.”

I accepted his greeting with a firm fist bump. “Dre. But, Abe. Now ain’t the time or place for one of yo’ pop up get rich schemes. Don’t call an-”

“What if I said make time?” Los interrupted.

“What if I said I’ll blow yo’ fucking face off?” I stepped up closer to him, devilishly smirking. “I’m the wrong nigga, bro. Abe you better get him. This ain’t that.”

“Dre. Chill, bro. This my cousin. You know what, you’re right. Now ain’t the time. Let’s bounce.” Abe pushed his cousin back, leading the crew back toward the cars.

Abe stopped short. “Dre. I was just checking in. Thought I could help. Bro.”

“Just be careful of the company you keep. And keep them away from our trap.” I warned.

Abe looked off. “Real talk, bro. I got a bad feeling about them. Like some shit waiting to jump off. I’m gon’ get my shit together, bro. Get back to the bag, shit prolly settle down with Yonni and get the fuck on.”

“What?” I had to laugh.

“Yeah, man. Every time I try to get up with another hoe, she end up popping up or I can't stop comparing them anyway. I think I love that girl."

"You should have been wifed her. Yonni a good chick."

"Look at you. Trying to be bros for real. I knew them ma'fuckas looked alike. Not that I was looking at Ox like that."

I had to laugh. "Shiiit, Ox that deal. I'd be looking too. Just don't touch."

"Whatever nigga. I'm out."

We gave a pound, then shoulder bumped. I called after him. "Aye, nigga. Be careful. If you need me. You already know."

***

"Who came to kiss and touch? Not me. Who came to beat it up? Rocky..."

The melody of Tank blasted threw the house and the smell of OG kush mixed with some of that oil burning from the Muslim cat at the gas station on Dexter and Joy Road met me at the door. I smiled because it was the perfect set up to come home to. I followed the sound of the music upstairs to the only room glowing with candles.

Damn. Ox was looking amazing, standing there in my wife beater and boy shorts. Her hair was a wild bush on top of her head and her face was glowing. My woman was bad as fuck.

I ran my tongue across my lips as I stared at her. “What you sitting all pretty in the dark for? Lighting candles, playing fuck me music by yourself and shit?”

“Because. I want you to do it to me.” She smiled. I had never heard Ox talk like that. I thought I was hearing wrong.

I laughed. “Whaaat?”

“You heard me. I want you to do it to me.” She repeated that shit. Ox was serious.

“Nah, kids do it. What I’m want to do is make love to you. Then fuck the shit out you.” Ox turned and looked away. “Nah, don’t be acting all shy now. Say it. Say it again. Tell me what you want me to do.”

“I want to make love to you. I want to feel you inside me. I want you to kiss me everywhere and tell me everything is okay. I want to feel like a woman and be okay with it. I just want you to fuck away my pain.” Ox confessed. I had never heard her sound so vulnerable. She admitted that like her life depended on it.

I walked up on her, pressing my body against hers. "Don't play these types of games with me Ox. I've been waiting patiently to feel yo' walls. But baby girl, I'll break your back playing it like this."

Ox blushed. "Don't break my back. I want it gentle. Love, not fucking."

I smirked, is that right? My hand fell to her left nipple. I caressed it, staring into her eyes. You know it's really a wrap if I slide inside you. This my shit already, but you gon' seal your fate. I'll kill you and whatever nigga brave enough to touch what's mine."

"Picture that. Why would that even be a factor, DeAndre? Stop ruining the mood. I geeked myself up to do this and I want to before I chicken out."

I laughed at the pout on her lips before kissing them. It started as a peck, but quickly escalated to an aggressive, passionate lip lock. I lifted her body from the ground, carrying her to the bed and gently laying her down.

Her hips spread beautifully across the bed, playing peek-a-boo in my wife beater. I swear, my dick was so hard that it felt like it was about to break. I had never gone more than a week without pussy. But, for Ox, I ignored my urges, going celibate for over six months. So, hell yeah o wanted to be a savage. But, Ox was special. I had to take my time with the pussy, treat it like a delicate flower, taste it like it was fine wine, and suck on it like a lollipop.

Using one hand to pull her panties down and the other to push her back, I took in her pretty pussy. It had never been entered. She was like a foreign land that only I would have the pleasure of exploring. I smirked. I was about to turn her little ass out.

I sucked her clit into my mouth, twirling my tongue around it, teasing her bud. Ox began to squirm. I hadn't even began yet. Sucking harder on her clit, I used two fingers to caress the entrance to her pot of gold. "That feels good to that lil' pussy, huh?"

She didn't respond with words. Instead, Ox let out a wounded cry. Ox's pussy tasted so pure that I could feast on it all night if she could take it. She was a runner, though. I gripped her hips and sucked on her pussy until her body froze and began to shake. She blessed me with her nectar and I'll be damned if it didn't take just like honey.

"Shit, DeAndre!" She called out. "What are you doing? I can't take it!"

"Oh, you gon' take it all, Ox. Do you know how long I've been waiting for this shit? I know you gon' let me fuck you how I want to fuck you."

I pulled my shirt over my head, unbuckling my jeans. Ox watched me, wide eyed and curious. When my boxers fell and my dick sprung to life, standing straight up, her eyes bugged.

She shook her head. "Unt uhh, DeAndre. I change my mind. You're going to hurt me."

I could see the fear in her eyes as she battled with her lust. Ox wanted it just as bad as I did, but I understood her apprehension.

"Relax, Ox. We're too far gone to turn back now. Let me have my pussy. I swear it's going to be like crack."

"Crack?"

"Hell yeah. You ever tried it?" I teased to lighten the mood, climbing on top of her.

"No, silly," She giggled.

"Right, I ain't never tried that either but I imagine that's what this dick like." I pressed the tip into her tight walls. Her shit was so tight that I could barely get in. Before she could screamed out, crushed my mouth into hers, kissing her passionately as my dick slowly dug it's way home.

I swear, Ox's pussy was my new home. The passion of our connection felt like I stuck a live electrical wire in a pool of water. I had only wiggled the tip in and it felt like we were raising off the bed.

Instead of forcing my way inside, I let her decide how much of this strong and long she was willing to endure by allowing her to control the mechanics of my hips with her hands. I didn’t want to force her. I didn’t want to be too much and scare her away either. So, I gave it to her slow and steady, allowing our bodies to rock to her rhythm.

Ox had a nigga open. I wanted to lay up in her pussy forever as I stared into her face. I never closed my eyes, admiring ever inch of her. Every face she made during and after ever stroke. I was the teacher and the student, learning the ways Oxtavia's body worked.

Chapter Twenty

Abe

Somerset was packed and I was annoyed as fuck. Yonni had me on this fuck boy, mushy shit. Ever since I told her I loved her, she had been using it against me. Had me spending time with her, doing couple shit.

“Ooh, Abraham! Aren’t these cute?” She held up a couple of Nike onesies and I frowned. We were inside Macy's. Yonni had me in every store in this mall and I was ready to go home and lay up in some pussy.

“Man, Yon, let’s go. You playing around now.” I switched the bags I had been carrying for her from hand to the other.

“But what if I’m not. What if I’m pregnant?” Her sparkling hazels settled on me. I didn’t know if she was fucking with my head or really trying to tell me something. With any other broad, the thought of them carrying my seed would have scared me. Honestly, with Yonni I didn’t care either way.

“Then you’d be pregnant, nigga. Let’s go.”

“Soooo, you wouldn’t be mad?”

“Nah, Yonni. When you fuck, you risk getting pregnant. What I’m going to be mad for?”

She smiled. “Good, because I’m pregnant.”

Pregnant? I’d be a lie if I said I wasn’t shocked. But nah, I wasn’t mad.

Yonni frowned. "So, you have nothing to say? Talk to me, Abraham. I'm pregnant, scared to death, and silence isn't the reaction I expected."

Damn, Yonni was about to have my baby. I was about to be a father. This shit was crazy. "Look at yo' mad ass." I chuckled at her trying to be all dramatic. "I'm just shocked. Ain't no reason to be scared now. We been fucking like pornstars. I guess we got to deal with the results. I ain't shit, but I ain't no hoe ass nigga, Yon."

Deyonni jumped in my arms, kissing my cheek. "I'm so relieved. I braced myself for your ignorant ass. I was fully prepared to knock you out. Thank you for being mature."

"Nah you wasn't gon' knock shit out but this dick." I teased, shaking my head. "Damn, man. My pull out game weak as fuck."

Yonni laughed as my hands fell on her ass. "That usually happens when the pussy good."

"You sound crazy, girl." I frowned. "Pussy ain't never stopped me from pulling out or strapping up. I don't fuck raw. I fucks with you heavy, though. It's only right I be the nigga you need me to be."

"Like, you love me?" Yonni's brow raised.

"You know I love yo' crazy ass. How can I not?"

Yonni opened her mouth to say something, but she was cut off. "You love her?" Neisha cocked her head to the side. "Did you love her before or after you manipulated me to give away my body?"

I ran my hand over my face. Neisha was turning into a straight psycho. I had a million calls and texts from her. I ignored them all. I mean, I had sympathy for her feeling used. But she made that decision to give her body to a nigga. “I didn’t put a gun to your head Neish.”

“You didn’t have to. You put a lie in my heart and it was just as fatal.” She smiled, looking crazy as hell. “But every dog has its day.” Neisha didn’t say nothing else. She walked off so smooth. I would be a lie if I said it didn’t rub me wrong.

“Do you even care about what you did to that girl?” Yonni's voice snapped me out of my thoughts.

“Man, fuck her. She's a grown ass woman. I didn’t force her to do nothing.” I was so glad that Yonni left it alone. I had a baby to worry about now.

***

After dropping Deyonni off, I had to shoot a few moves and ended up pulling up on my cousin Los at his lounge. I didn’t plan to be out long. Yonni was waiting up for me and she had already sent me those freaky ass pictures playing in her pussy.

I smirked, finally deciding to stop fighting her crazy ass. I told her I would try the couple's thing since we was bonded forever now. Surprisingly, it felt good knowing I would be going home to my woman.

I tapped Los, standing to head to the bar. “I’m about to get a drink, then I’m out bro. You be careful out here.”

Los smiled. “I’m always careful, soft ass nigga. When you ready to get some real money, holla at me. Get your feelings out your ass. These hoes gon’ fuck for free. We might as well get paid for it.”

I nodded. “I feel you. Different strokes for different folks. I'm good at slinging dope, not pussy.”

I slapped fives with my cousin before making my way to the bar. Being locked in with him felt nothing like being with my bros. They had my back and I knew without a shadow of doubt I was good with them. But with Los, I just had this negative energy looming around me.

I side stepped through the crowd, making it to the bar, leaning against it. “Let me get a Remy and Coke.” I ordered my drink, staring at the bartender's fat ass. Damn, being a one woman's man was about to be a challenge. I shook my head as my body tensed, feeling the heat from a body too close.

“I loved you. But every dog has its day.” The warm air from her breath made the hairs on my neck stand up. I never got a chance to turn around to face Neisha. I felt the cold steel of the knife tear into my flesh. I tried to get her off of me, but it kept ripping into my skin. I thought about Yonni and my baby. I thought about the change that I was planning to make. It was slowly fading away. Everything faded away.

Chapter Twenty-One

Cam

I couldn't believe that someone took Abe. That shit was so unreal. It didn't even feel right to stand over his casket and watch him being lowered into the ground. My chest tightened as I thought about the funeral the day before. That had to be the toughest shit I ever experienced. My heart went out to Yonni, though. She had a breakdown so bad that she ended up having to be taken to the hospital in an ambulance.

I tried my best to shake the emotions that were threatening to spill out. Dexter had taken so much from us and I knew that if we didn't make it out the hood, and soon, we would never make it out. Too much toxicity was imbedded in the streets.

"Are you okay, Camden?" Kelsey's soft voice interrupted my train of thoughts. Never in a million years would I have thought the first person I ran to after my best friend was murdered would be her. The reality was, we both were hurting. She lost a brother and I did too. Life was too short to be worried about what ma'fuckas thought.

I smiled over at Kelsey. "Yeah, I'm straight. I'll be good. Thank you."

Her lips formed a pout. "Are you sure it's a good idea for me to be with you? There's so much bad blood. Emotions are racing right now. I mean, I can't honestly say that I'm at peace with what happened to my brother. I don't understand it. I don't even understand my emotions for you. But, I love you Camden and it feels like you're all I have right now." Her eyes glazed with tears, but they didn't fall.

I nodded. I didn't understand what we were doing either, but I knew she put me at peace, so I didn't give a damn who liked her riding next to me or not.

We rode in silence for the majority of the ride. The kids were in the backseat watching the tablet, and my mind was heavy. After the get together, Kelsey, me, and the kids had a flight scheduled to Florida. Today would be our last day in Michigan. We had to let the chaos go and start over. There wasn't any other choice.

I had a few dollars saved up from hustling, and Kelsey's brother left behind a fortune. We were set up to live comfortably for a very long time and we both needed it more than life.

My eyes slanted back to the kids. I couldn't believe how the cookie crumbled. However, with Tiff possibly about to do a long bid, I had no other a choice but to man up. They were my hearts and they didn't have anyone else. There was no way I was allowing them to get put in the system. Tiff's people weren't shit and she probably didn't know who their daddies were.

What was even more crazy, Kelsey accepted them with open arms. I wasn't no good this past week. But, she was there feeding me and the kids.

Pulling up to Ox and Dre's house, I killed the engine. "There ain't no need for explanations. I want you here and that's all that matters. Come on," I opened my door and she followed with Sha and Trey behind her, we met up at the sidewalk, holding hands until we made it inside the apartment.

We were supposed to be having a get together to celebrate Abe, but the energy in the room was solemn. Ox was consoling Yonni, Dre and Deek were kicking it with a few homies from the hood, and Cherish just sat to herself.

Kelsey squeezed my hand. “Are you sure I should be here?” She asked again.

I squeezed her hand back for reassurance. “If you ain’t allowed to be here, I ain’t either. Chill.” I guided her and the kids to seats ducked off in the corner.

Then, I made my way to the crew, slapping fives with Rah, Dre, then the rest of them. It felt weird as hell to be together without Abe.

Dre tapped me, nodding toward Kelsey. “Why she here bro?” He frowned. “We dealing with enough shit to be having random broads around.”

I cocked my head, taking a step back. “What? I just lost my nigga. You fucked with Abe, but that was my motherfuckin' brother! I don’t give a fuck about that other shit. She here because I want her to be. That’s why.” I snapped, as everything began to hit me at once. All the bottled up emotions I had been experiencing settled in my chest and were racing to spill out.

Dre pointed to the door. “She got to go,”

“Nah nigga. She ain’t got to go nowhere. She lost a whole brother behind you nigga. Every action has a reaction and it all started from you,” I pointed out. “You killed Q and got that nigga Rick beefing with us. That beef tore us all apart. We almost lost Ox, we lost a brother behind this shit too. Fuck that petty shit you talking." My voice was a little louder than needed, but I couldn't control it.

"So you trying to say I killed Abe, nigga?"

"Nah, I'm trying to say ain't nobody an angel but it ain't shit we can do about it. We coming together for Abe. Fuck the bullshit."

Kelsey walked over to me with the kids in tow. Her tiny hand rested on mine. "It's okay, Camden. Me and the kids will wait in the car."

"Nah, you ain't going nowhere."

"Will y'all stop!" Yonni hopped up screaming. "I buried my soulmate yesterday. I don't want to hear that shit. What about... what about me!" She banged on her chest as a deeply rooted cry escaped. Cherish rushed to her side, pulling Yonni into a hug.

Yonni snatched away. "No! You never liked Abraham in the first place! You don't care." She was hysterical and I felt bad for getting into it with Dre over bullshit.

Cherish rubbed her back and we all watched the mother and daughter display of affection. "I care, Yonni. I never wanted my grandchild to be without a father. I never wanted to see my daughter hurting so badly. I care."

Grandchild?

Ox said what everybody was thinking. "You're pregnant, Yonni?"

Deyonni shook her head. "Yessss. He promised me that he was ready to do things the right way. We were finally going to have our happily ever after and some emotional bitch took him from me." Her chest heaved as she cried. "This is killing me and the last thing I want to hear is fighting when I'm in a constant battle with myself."

Both Cherish and Ox embraced Yonni in a three-way hug. I felt my chest tighten, like I was suffocating. I turned to Kelsey. "Our time is up. We have to go so we can make that flight. We have to get the fuck out of here." I literally couldn't breathe and I knew that things wouldn't be right until I was off Dexter, out of Michigan, and far away from all the chaos it brought.

Chapter Twenty-Two

Dre

Four months later...

Making the move to Virginia was bittersweet for us. We needed the new start, but the circumstances that brought us to the beach was fucked up. Losing Abe took its toll on everyone. But, we were finally picking up the pieces and starting to get our life back in order.

Cherish wasn't playing when she said she would look out. She gave me a seat at the table and we were eating like we never ate before, with no drama. Well, we had a few misunderstandings here and there but we were good.

The connection that Ox and I had was what made it perfect. She didn't have to hide behind rules no more. When she smiled, it was genuine. She was the purest thing I had in my life... plus her pussy was magical.

The ladies sat at the crib and did girl shit, while Rahdeek and I held it all down. Business had been crazy, so I hadn't been able to chill with Ox as much as I wanted to. That's what today was about. I took it off to celebrate her.

We were walking the boardwalk on Virginia Beach. It smelled like fresh seaweed, ice cream, and freedom.

"You think you're slick, DeAndre. I know why you being all nice. I told you, I don't celebrate birthdays." Ox rolled her eyes, looping her arm around mine.

She was rocking this form-fitting maxi dress. Her hair was pressed and hanging down her back, and that ass was looking right. I loved Ox in any form I could have her. But, being around the ladies, it had her softening, and blossoming into a woman. Man, I didn't think it was physically possible for her to look any better, but my baby was mean with it.

I smiled at her. "Nah, you used to not celebrate it. Now, you got every reason to celebrate living. I'm gon' always make you feel special for blessing me with another year."

"Listen to you talkin' like you talkin'. You know you was already getting some. You don't have to butter me up." Ox teased. Her eyelashes fluttered, giving off a soft feminine vibe.

"That's a fact, my baby. Whenever and however I want it. I'm speakin' truths, though. I'm gon' give you the world and if I can't afford it, I'll take that shit for you."

Before Ox could respond, my phone buzzed with a Facetime from Cam. The nigga was always on the go. There wasn't no telling where he was callin' me from.

"What's up, bro?" I answered, holding the phone to my face. I had to laugh at this goofy nigga. He had the camera on his feet, sitting in sand.

"You see that," Cam spoke. "That's a nigga with no worries. Sand between the toes and shit." He teased, flipping the camera to his face. "What you know about these palms trees and half naked br-"

Kelsey tapped him. “Watch your mouth, Camden.”

He chuckled. “I’m just playing baby. You the only half naked queen I see.” He was laying it on thick and I was just digging the natural smile that we all rocked. Dexter Ave was the jungle and we made it out that ma'fucka.

“Soft ass nigga. What’s up Kels?” I spoke. I respected her as Cam's girl, but I could never see us being close. There was too much bad blood associated with her. Quite frankly, I couldn’t trust a broad that fucked with the enemy over her blood anyway. But, I wasn’t the one fucking her, so it didn’t make me no difference.

“Hey DeAndre.” She smiled into the camera. “Your boy and the babies are about to drive me crazy. He's lucky Sha is my little best friend.”

That was another thing that blew me. It was also the reason I gave Kels a pass. She accepted another broad's babies as her own. Like I said, it wasn’t for me to dissect. So, if Cam liked it, I loved it.

I shrugged. “It be like that sometimes.” I turned to Ox, she was staring ahead, almost as if she was daydreaming. I tapped her. “You good, beautiful? You never said what up to Cam.”

Ox smiled. “Heyyyy, Cam. We miss you.” She cooed.

“We?” A brow raised.

“Yes, we. You cry every other day about how much you miss your bro. We need to link up somewhere like old times.”

Cam nodded, squinting in the camera. “Yeah, we can make that happen soon. I’m gon' get the fam together and make a trip to VA.”

“That’s what up. Be safe, bro. These streets cold.”

He smirked. “That’s why I’m not in ‘em no more. I’ll leave that to them other niggas. I do real estate. Go to work and come home to my family every day.”

“That’s the way to be, bro. Be easy.”

We ended the Facetime call. Ox was staring at me. “I have to ask God to work with me with that girl. She's cool, but I just don’t like her.”

“Yeah, she cool. I really don’t give a fuck though. I wake up to yo' pretty ass every day, so it don’t make me no difference.”

Ox blushed. “I hear you.” She leaned in and kissed me.

“Nah, I want you to feel me. I need you to always feel me.”

***

Every Sunday, Cherish did the family thing. She did the big dinner, music, and cards. Rahdeek and Cherish were cool as hell. We had our moments, but I fucked with them the long way. I ain’t never had no father figure. I looked up to Rah. He kept it one thousand, and gave that good wise advice.

I saw why Cherish was digging him. He was a protector, a provider, and a leader. But, he also knew how to balance it out. I learned a lot from him, because balance was something Ox and I needed. Her being kidnapped did something to me. I wanted to always be able to protect her. So, I overdid it sometimes.

"Why y'all playing this sad ass music." I walked into the house. It smelled like fresh spice and fried chicken. I never walked into a place and it just felt like home. Cherish's house felt like home.

"No, why you got your shoes on in my house, DeAndre? I done told you about that a million times."

"You worse than them old folks." I chuckled, pulling my Jordans off. Cherish stayed in a big ass eight bedroom house in Chesapeake, VA. She had plush white carpet, nice ass Italian leather furniture, and she was big on decorations. Pictures and plants were everywhere.

"Whatever," She turned to Yonni who was sitting on the couch. I felt bad for Sis. Ever since Abe passed, she wasn't herself. Yonni was crazy as fuck, but she was quiet these days. "You want to go to the store with me, Yonni? We can get the baby some butter pecan ice cream."

"No, I'm fine ma. You know you don't have to baby me. I'm good, really." She smiled and Ox went to go sit next to her. They were almost inseparable.

I watched Cherish watch them. She seemed so at peace. I thought about my mother and tried not to feel no type of way. She finally found her peace and they took her.

You knew what you was doing God. I thought, deciding to find Rah. I knew he was in the den smoking a cigar and I needed a little man talk.

"Deek. What's the deal?" We smacked fives as I sat down next to him.

“I can’t call it. Trying to enjoy this off day. The bag is in. We got product to move.”

“You know I’m always ready. But fuck that. I need yo' advice. I’m trying to marry Ox. Fuck playing house if I know I’m gon' die loving that girl. I don’t be wanting to smother her though.”

Rahdeek chuckled. “So, you trying to put the pressure on all us? Everybody gon' be thinkin' they need a ring.”

“They deserve it. Don’t they?” I asked, taking a shot. Cherish and Deek had been together over ten years and hadn’t made it official.

Rahdeek shrugged. “It ain’t me. Cherish is stubborn as hell. I love her to death, but it’s a power thing. I ain’t tripping. When Cherish ready to take my last name, we'll make it right. But, in the meantime, make Ox official. She loves you.”

I tapped my pocket for the little velvet box that held our future. Today was the day God blessed the earth with Ox. She hated her birthday, but I wanted to give her a reason to celebrate it every year going forward. I needed to reshape her memories of the day she was born. We were given a new beginning and I’d be damned if we didn’t live it up to the fullest. Living our happily ever after was better than busting a nut.

Epilogue

Ox

We hadn't been back to the city in years. Riding through the hood didn't even feel the same. I didn't miss Detroit and I for damn sure didn't get all fuzzy inside as we rode up Dexter and into our old hood. I bit down on my bottom lip, staring at Dre. I knew that no man was perfect, but he was the closest thing to perfection that I was getting... perfectly imperfect.

"You hungry, fat momma?" His brown eyes settled on me, sending a shiver up my spine. Got damn, he touched my entire being without actually touching me.

I smiled. "Ain't I'm always hungry? This baby is going to have me fat as a house." My lips poked out. "I'm about to be somebody's mother, Dre."

"I know. And you gon' be the best mother alive." He assured me, placing his hand on my knee. I heard a lot of women say that they married their best friend. Shit, Dre was more than my best friend. He was my everything all wrapped into one. Moving to Virginia and giving my mother a chance had to be the best decision of both of our lives because it gave us a chance to survive, love, and be loved.

"Thank you, babe. You're going to be the best father too. Our little family is all we got."

"No it ain't. Little nigga gon' be surrounded by love. Spoiled as fuck, just like yo' nephew."

My lips formed a point. Being in the city and thinking about Yonni and Abe's son made my heart drop. He was supposed to be alive experiencing the peace that we had. Yonni wasn't supposed to be a single parent.

"I miss him, Dre. Abe didn't deserve that." I spoke in a low whisper. "I don't want to be here long. It brings back too many bad memories. The vibe isn't even the same."

Dre licked his lips as we turned down h9is mother's old block. "Nah, I fuck with the city because it reminds me of who I was and who I ain't gon' be no more." We pulled right in front of her apartment building.

My eyes squinted as the sun beamed down on us. The mural for Ronnie was still up. Flowers and teddy bears were hung on the light pole across from where Dre's mother was murdered at.

I watched as Dre grabbed the fresh flowers and bear that we had gotten to add to the mural. His face was stoic, but I knew that dealing with Ronnie's death was still a battle he was trying to get used to.

He stood outside, his held bowed. I knew he was praying. Dre had evolved a lot from the man that didn't trust God. He was a praying man now. Dre was nowhere near the wild, lost soul he was just a few years ago.

I smiled. Mrs. Thompson wouldn't have allowed him to stay the same. She was our blessing. She never had kids and she didn't have much family, but she accepted us in like we were hers. They say God put people in your life for a reason and a season. I knew exactly why we crossed paths. We needed each other.

My smiled widened. I knew she was going to be so shocked to see us here in the city. She had visited Virginia a couple of times over the years, but we had never been back.

I watched as Dre hung his gifts for his mother, rubbing my stomach. I was seven months pregnant I could only pray that I was everything this baby needed. I wanted to shower her with love, because Lord knows neither of us had it growing up, I needed to school her on this crazy world and let her know that she wasn't alone. I needed for Dre and I to be everything we never had growing up.

"I thought I was going to be fucked up. But, I'm at peace, Ox. Thank you for being my peace. We free, babe. He took in a deep breath. We made it off the block. We living, my baby." He gripped my hand. "I love you 'til I can't love you no more and even then, I'll find a way to love you harder."

My heart melted. Dre gave me goosebumps . "I love you too DeAndre." Leaning over, I kissed my man. This was definitely what peace felt like. I never thought I'd experience it, but I was free.

***

Deyonni

"Ayonni! Get over here boy!" I yelled as my son ran off, giggling. He was hardheaded just like his daddy and his little face was the splitting image of that man. Two years had passed since Abraham was taken away from us. Sometimes it still stung, but I was finally coming to terms with everything.

"Stop yelling at my grandson," My mother giggled. We were at the beach, enjoying a little family time. We had always been close but the baby and having Ox around made us closer. She loosened the ropes around me and let me be me. I think having our family be complete finally eased her.

I rolled my eyes. "That's his problem. Between you, Ox, and Dre, I don't know who has him more rotten. That's why he's so hardheaded now. He's spoiled." I began to run after him, he was getting too far. "Come back here, Ayonni!"

"Ayon-" My words were cut off as I bumped into a hard chest. I fell back a little, but strong arms gripped me up."

"Whoa, be careful beautiful." The voice was a sexy rasp. My eyes traveled up his frame and when I landed on his face, I almost fainted. I had to do a double take. The man's features reminded me so much of Abe.

I felt my adrenaline rushing as I stepped around him. "I'm... I'm sorry." I walked off, speed walking to Ayonni and snatching his little arm up.

My emotions were all over the place. They say everybody had a twin in the world and I cursed my luck for having to run into Abe's. It brought back emotions I thought I had buried. Abe was the only man that I'd ever really loved. I didn't know what it was that had me open from the first night he tried to run game on me.

I giggled. Abraham was such a whore. But, he met his match with me. The chase was fun and when I finally got him to submit and be the man I needed him to be, some bitch took him.

"I don't even do this," There was that raspy voice again. "But, I can't walk by without telling you how beautiful you are. You should let me take you out."

"I don't do strangers," I shot back.

"I'm only a stranger because you not trying to let me in, ma. I bet you ain't never had a d-boy. Fuck around and change your life." His up north accent was thick and sexy, going right along with the dimple in his smile.

My nose crinkled. "Where are you from?"

"Detroit. I been in VA a couple years, though. Searching for my future. I finally found her too."

I giggled, as Ayonni began to squirm. "It must be a Detroit thing, because y'all niggas are cocky." I lifted my son, holding him in my arms. At two, he was a busy body.

"What you know about Detroit, ma?"

"Enough," I stared this total stranger down, hating that feeling that he gave off. He reminded me so much of Abraham that it was scary. "His father was from Detroit."

"Lucky man. Where he at now so I can congratulate him?"

"He was murdered before I had my son," I answered solemnly.

"Sorry to hear that," He looked off.

"No need to be. What's your name?"

"Santiago. But you can call me Sunny." He smiled. "Or you can call me the future. I'm good at taking shit and I'm plotting on your heart right now as we speak."

I chuckled. "What? You don't even know me."

"That's fine. I ain't got to know you to know what I want." He pulled out his phone. "Put your number in here. Let me take you out to eat so I can tell you how I'm about to steal your soul."

I had to shake my head because I knew I had no business smiling in this man's face. I wasn't in the right space to fall in love or date. But, something deep down was telling me I had to let Abraham go and be happy again.

After reading off my number and him saving it. I watched as he pulled out a wad of cash and peeled off a twenty. "Here, go get my lil' man an ice cream and make sure you answer that ma'fuckin phone when I call."

His aggressiveness was so sexy to me. I could tell we were going to have fun with our power struggle. I was so used to being in charge.

I smiled, watching him walk off. Then, I looked to the sky. "I guess you found a way to get back to me, Lil' Nuts. He ain't you, but he'll do for now. I miss you, baby."

A single tear slid down my cheek, but Ayonni wiped it away before I could. "No crying mommy. Be a big girl." His little voice was so cute.

I kissed his forehead. "Mommy isn't crying. I'm happy."

He wrapped his tiny arms around my neck, giving me the best baby hug. "I love you too, mommy."

I released a sigh of relief. I was content. I didn't understand the way of the world, but I was still happy all the same.

***

Cam

"Stop running so fast, Camden! I can't keep up!" Kelsey yelled.

I had to laugh at her short legs and big belly. My baby was trying her hardest to keep up. "Run faster," I yelled behind me, purposely leaving her.

I had something special planned for today, so I wanted to make sure everything was right. Kelsey and I had been through straight hell and back. We had to deal with death, betrayal, hurt, pain... shit, I had been through it all with her and that's what made me love her so much.

Kels was special. She accepted me at my worst. She accepted Tiff's kids like her own, helping me raise them until Tiff's ten year bid was up. Most importantly, she loved me unselfishly after all the bullshit we went through.

Finally making it back to the house from our jog, my eyes traveled to where Sha and her brother were hiding. Sha's goofy ass had this big, silly grin plastered across her face and lil' Trey just stood there, unbothered as hell. Lil' man was the chillest eight year old I knew.

I winked at them before turning to Kelsey, watching as she pulled herself and my baby inside her belly to the house. "It's fucked up you just left me like that Camden!" She fussed, slapping her knees to catch her breath.

I smirked. "I was just seeing if you was willing to follow me across the world, baby."

"What? How does you leaving me behind in a jog have anything to do with where I'm following you? I'm mad at you." Her lips poked out and I stepped forward to kiss them.

I wrapped my arms around her. "Because just like you was determined to keep up with me on that jog, I know you willing to keep up in this crazy ass life. I know I'm willing to follow you to the end of the world and back, Kels. You opened my eyes to a lot of shit. I was lost before I found you. I'm a new man because of you. I don't want to bring my baby into the world without you having my last name."

Kelsey took a step back covering her face. "What are you saying Abraham?"

I smiled, winking at Sha and Trey. They were hiding on the other side of 1

the tree behind Kelsey. I waited for them to creep up before I dropped on one knee.

"Will you marry my uncle?" Both Sha and Trey said in unison. Kelsey whipped around toward them, before focusing on me again. It took forever for me to find the perfect ring to fit Kelsey's finger. Ordinary wasn't good enough for her. She deserved the world and I was going to give it to her. I was no longer that lil' nigga trapped on Dexter Ave. I was a grown as man ready to do grown things.

A brow raised, "So you gon' let me give you my last name or not?"

Kelsey nodded. “Yes! Of course, Camden.” I placed the ring on her finger and we all hugged. Sha, Trey, me, and Kelsey. The ride was crazy as fuck, but I wouldn’t change it for the world.

Made in the USA
Monee, IL
13 February 2020

21766637R00090